Self Reflection

by

David McCormac

In loving memory of Kevin the cat.

Contents

The Death of a Duke

Characters

The New Duke
A small weak looking man who is the twin brother of Michael.
Life has left him very bitter. He hates Mo with a passion.

Other Characters
Mo, Phoebe, Mini Meg, Lord Fircum, Duke and Duchess of
Ruttingham. Michael, chauffeur, vicar and Lady Bet.

Setting
The church, Mo's cottage.

The Death of a Duke

Mo and Phoebe are standing outside the church on a cold January morning.

Mo
He was a wonderful man.

Phoebe
He was, inside and out. Is Michael bringing the family with him?

Mo
No, he is just bringing himself. The children have both got the flu, so Jane is staying at home.

Phoebe
Coming out in this weather wouldn't help their health.

Lady Bet is walking up the church path.

Lady Bet
Hello you wonderful person.

Mo
Hello Lady Bet, it's wonderful to see you again. *(They both hug)*

Lady Bet
Well a sad day, but not an unexpected one. He had a very good life and that was partially down to you.

Mo
This is Phoebe Dickinson, a dear friend.

Lady Bet
Hello my dear. Do you know, I can see both love and pain in

your eyes. Whoever it is, don't let them get away. *(Turning back to Mo)* After the service I'm getting straight off. The thought of stepping into a house where my nephew is in charge, makes me shudder. *(Handing a letter to Mo)* I have written you a letter, stating what I want you to have when my time comes. I hope you love it as much as I have. *(She kisses Mo and walking into the church. Mo puts the letter into her pocket)*

Phoebe
Can you see the love and pain in my eyes?

Mo
I can see the make-up is getting thicker *(they both laugh)* But there is something that is bothering you.

Phoebe
I'm starting to fall in love with him and yes before you say it, he is half my age and yes he only sees me as his mistress, but Mo I can't stop my feelings.

Mo
Have you told him how you feel?

Phoebe
To hear the word no from him would break me. Mo, what am I going to do?

Mo
You're going to leave it with me.

Phoebe
But Mo.

Mo
How many years have you known me?

Phoebe

Over forty years.

Mo

Then trust me.

The Duke and Duchess of Ruttingham come up the church path. The Duke walks straight into the church, but the Duchess stops.

The Duchess

Hello Mo, it's been a long time.

Mo

Too long Brenda. How are things?

The Duchess

Things are going well, especially now the Duke has stopped climbing on top of me.

Mo

Why is that?

The Duchess

I've hidden his Viagra pills. So there's no point. *(They both laugh)*

Mo

Are you still getting your bush clipped?

The Duchess

I have had to employ another gardener. My bush is now a two man job.

Mo

No wonder you have got an athletic figure.

The Duchess

I'm running a marathon a week *(laughing)* I'll see you later. *(She walks into the church)*

Phoebe

I can see she has gone down a couple of dress sizes.

Mo

Well, she is working out a lot. Watch out, here comes the lecherous lord.

Lord Fircum

Miss Moore. How wonderful to see you.

Mo

Thank you your Lordship, but it's Mrs Johnson now. I got married.

Lord Fircum

What a lucky fella. You and your husband must come and stay with me for a weekend. You will be my special guests.

Mo

That is so kind of you. We must sort something out.

Lord Fircum

Now don't forget. I'll see you later. *(He kisses Mo's head and walks into the church)*

Phoebe

What was all that about?

Mo

His Lordship has taken up swinging.

Phoebe

Dirty perv.

(Mini Meg comes up the church path.)

Mini Meg

Good morning Mrs Johnson, good morning Mrs Dickson.

Mo/Phoebe

Good morning Meg.

Mo

How are things?

Mini Meg

Mrs Johnson, I'm rushed off my feet. What with the cookery class, weddings and funerals, I never stop.

Phoebe

How's Penny's fingers? Is she still wearing clear nail varnish?

Mini Meg

As far as I know.

Phoebe

What do you mean?

Mini Meg

Well, the other day I saw her scratching her top lip, which as you know is too close for comfort. So, as she is becoming familiar with that part of her face again, I thought it was best not to take any chances. So, I have put six plasters on each of her fingers, so if she thinks about putting her fingers up her nose, the thickness of the plasters will prevent her from doing so.

Phoebe
The last thing we want is for her to get her fingers up.

Mini Meg
I must go in and get a seat at the front, or I won't get to see anything. See you both later. *(She walks into the church)*

The Duke's chauffeur comes up the church path.

Chauffeur
Good morning Mrs Johnson.

Mo
Good morning. Are you still chauffeuring?

Chauffeur
No. As soon as the Duke died, I felt I couldn't go on, especially as the new Duke is not a person that deserves loyalty.

Mo
I know what you mean. But can I say a big thank you for your loyalty to the old Duke over so many years. Also, I would like to thank you for keeping him sexually active, right to the very end. I know that your mouth kept him happy for many a hour.

Chauffeur
To hear his moans of pleasure, was a great honour.

Mo
Giving your loyalty to the whole of his needs, is a rare thing and should be celebrated.

Chauffeur
Thank you Mrs Johnson. *(He walks into the church)*

Mo

Here comes the hearse. Right, come on, lets get ourselves in. The last person I want to see is the new Duke. *(Both Mo and Phoebe walk into the church and find themselves a seat)*

The coffin is carried in with the help of Michael. The rest of the Duke's family are seen walking behind. The new Duke glares distastefully as he spots Mo. The coffin is put down and the family sit down on the front pews.

Phoebe

(Whispering) If looks could kill you would be six foot under. He would love to dance on your grave.

Mo

I would like to see that, especially as I'm getting buried at sea.

Vicar

We come together today, to remember the life of a man who was so kind and generous to so many. He was known as a man who was always there for his friends and family night and day. The Duke was born on the fifth of November 1933.

Phoebe

(Whispering) I wondered what lit so many woman's fires.

Vicar

For much of his childhood, the Duke was schooled at Rideum High School. At eighteen he moved onto Oxford and studied English. At twenty-one, he left Oxford with a first and decided to travel around Europe. A year into his travels came the news that his father has died, making him the new Duke. A few years later, he met and marries the late Duchess, they had three children. James, Michael and Caroline. *(Phoebe squeezes Mo's hand)* Michael would now like to read a poem, in his father's memory.

Michael

(Standing up)
You will never be forgotten,
You will never say goodbye.
You were gone before I knew it,
And only God knew why.

A million times I needed you,
A million times I've cried.
If love alone could have saved you.
You never would have died.

In life I loved you dearly,
In death I love you still.
In my heart you hold a place,
That no-one could ever fill.

It broke my heart to lose you,
But you didn't go alone.
For part of me went with you,
The day God took you home.

Tears start to fall down Michael's cheeks as he sits down.

Vicar

Thank you Michael. We will sing: 'All things bright and beautiful'.

As they start to sing, the family follow the vicar to look at the flowers. Everyone follows suit. Looking at the arrangements, everyone commiserates with the family.

Phoebe

There's some nice wreaths. Even your small offering looks nice.

Mo
It's not all about the size.

Phoebe
You speak for yourself.

Michael comes up to his mother and hugs her.

Mo
How are you darling?

Michael
I'm bearing up. I was hoping to pop round and see you later, but by the time I've been to the family burial.

Mo
The next time you have a weekend free, pop up and we will have some quality time together.

Michael
That's a promise.

Mo
Can you do me a favour?

Michael
Of course.

Mo
Will you put this on your father's coffin for me?

Michael
Of course I will. I'll send him your love.

Mo
The new Duke looks pale.

Michael

With half his wine cellar being drunk already and the bad company he keeps all hours of the day and night, his health will only get worse.

Mo

Right, I better get this one home, her prodigy will be freaking out without guidance.

Michael

Does she ever change?

Mo

Not as long as I've known her. That's why she is as dear to me now as she was then. Bye bye my love. *(They kiss and hug each other, then Michael walks away)* Right Phoebe Dickson, are you ready?

Phoebe

I wonder if I'll get such beautiful flowers at my funeral.

Mo

I shouldn't think so. You were deflowered years ago.

They both walk down the church path and along the lane. They reach Mo's cottage.

Phoebe

Right, I'll see you later.

Mo

Will you come in? I need to tell you something that has been a secret for the last thirty years.

Phoebe

That sounds troubling.

They both go inside, where Mo puts the kettle on and Phoebe sits in the living room. Ten minutes later Mo brings in the tea and puts the tray on the table. As she does this, she starts to cry.

Mo
I'm sorry.

Phoebe
Right, get yourself sat down next to me and tell me what's the problem.

Mo
(Wiping away her tears) James.

Phoebe
James, the new Duke?

Mo
Yes.

Phoebe
What about him?

Mo
He is...

Phoebe
He is what? Come on, spit it out.

Mo
He is my son.

Phoebe
Are you saying you got pregnant a second time?

21

Mo

No, just once.

Phoebe

You had twins?

Mo

Yes.

Phoebe

(Looking shocked) Bloody hell Mo, you are a dark horse. You better tell me what happened.

Mo

Well you know I was pregnant with Michael.

Phoebe

I did.

Mo

But unbeknownst to anyone there was another baby, that had tucked itself behind the other baby. It wasn't until I had about two weeks to go that the scan found a second child, that was much smaller and showing very little movement.

Phoebe

So what did the Duke say?

Mo

Like me he was very shocked. At the same time the Duchess was also pregnant, but with all her pregnancies she was unable to carry them full-term, having miscarries with everyone. With every miscarriage, the Duchess grew weaker, until it was decided that if her present pregnancy ended in failure, she would not try again. So the Duke hatched a plan to pass my twins off as the Duchesses.

Phoebe

Did the Duchess miscarry?

Mo

She did a day before I gave birth. The Duke sorted out all the paperwork and an hour later I had given birth. Lady Bet came round to collect my babies. When I handed them to her, I knew what hell was like. I stayed there for my years later.

Phoebe

Did you feel the same about both of them?

Mo

To be honest with you, when I looked into Michael's eyes my heart skipped a beat. He was everything I wanted in a son. But with James, I didn't feel that love and connection. But I will give the Duchess her due, knowing her own weakness and seeing the weakness of James, she took him straight away and never let him out of her sight. So it was many years before I saw him again.

Phoebe

So if the Duchess never had any children of her own, where did the daughter come from?

Mo

You remember Boozy Gill who always looked ill?

Phoebe

Yes.

Mo

Well, she went to a party, which coming from a very religious family was really unheard of for Gill. She was sitting there, drinking line and lemon with her friend when the Duke walked in. Well you know how charming and persistent the Duke was.

Phoebe
I know.

Mo
Well. Throughout the night he sent over drink after drink, but Gill wouldn't touch them. But finally, the Duke sent over a 'pink gin'.

Phoebe
Mother's ruin.

Mo
She crumbled and found herself in the Duke's hotel suite. Nine months later she gave birth to a girl in one of the Duke's cottages. Her parents disowned her and no man would come near her, so the deal was, that the Duke would let her stay in the cottage and pay all her bills if she gave the child up. She had no choice. The day she did so was the day that Mother's ruin locked in.

Phoebe
Poor, poor woman.

Mo
Now you know why she had a smile on her face when she died. Her suffering was at an end.

Phoebe
What about your suffering.

Mo
What I had to do will never leave me guilt free. But I do have one last dream.

Phoebe
What is it?

Mo

To see Michael become the Duke one day. After all he was the first born.

Phoebe

I'm sure that dream will be fulfilled. Especially as the present Duke continues to add to his poor health.

Mo

Only time will tell.

We Love You, Mr M

Characters

Mr M

A young good looking supply teacher who is celebrating his fortieth birthday. His theatrical teaching methods brings out the best in the children he teaches.

Miss Roach

A young woman in her twenties. She is around five foot ten in height and loves to party.

Miss Bigwood

A tall woman in her forties. She is the head teacher who has a no-nonsense attitude.

Mr Browny

A tall man in his early fifties, who thinks he is much younger. He is always up for a laugh and can bitch with the best of them.

Mr Woody

A part time teacher in his fifties. He is of medium height with a passion for boat building.

The children

Lucy, James, Gary, Caroline, Jeremy, Aegeus, Robert, Johnny, Mabel, Zeeta and Rita (twins), Valerie, Amy, David and Marvin. They are all between the ages of five and six.

Mrs Archer

A small woman in her thirties.

Charlie

A year six boy who is very street-wise.

Settings

A school classroom and a playing field.

We Love You Mr M

Mr M goes into a reception class at around eight in the morning. He sees Mo sitting at one of the children's desks.

Mr M

Well. Good morning to you.

Mo

Hello.

Mr M

You must be the volunteer for the morning.

Mo

Yes, I'm Mrs Johnson.

Mr M

Well, it's great to see you. My day has just got so much better. I'm Mr M, the humble supply. In fact, you couldn't get much humbler than me. So nice lady, what brings you here today?

Mo

My ward, Billy, in year 5, keeps on at me to do a bit of voluntary work. So, I thought I would pop in for a morning and lend a hand.

Mr M

That's so kind of you. In fact, I'm only here this morning myself. It's my birthday today, so it's a party night tonight. It's not every day you reach forty.

Mo

Did you say forty?

Mr M

I did.

Mo

I would have put you nearer thirty.

Mr M

You sweet talking devil you. I know we are going to get on just fine. Have you got any children of your own?

Mo

Well, of course. I've got Billy now and one other.

Mr M

Of course. That was a wonderful thing you did.

Mo

Well, when a dying woman comes to you and asks you to take care of her children, the word no is not an option. Although there were times I could have easily walked away,

Mr M

Why didn't you?

Mo

When you look into a dying mother's eyes and the only thing that is keeping them open is the anguish and desperation of seeing that your children will be cared for when you have gone, makes you continue. You know your pain is nothing compared to what she was suffering. Although, when you have a child like Billy, it is so worth everything I went through.

Mr M

You are truly blessed.

Five minutes later, the classroom door opens and in walks the

teaching assistant Miss Roach.

Miss Roach
Morning everyone.

Mr M
Here comes the living dead. Did you go out last night Miss Roach?

Miss Roach
You are loud this morning Mr M.

Mr M
You are hungover Miss Roach. Where did you go?

Miss Roach
A new club has opened up, 'Brewers Drake'.

Mr M
That's ironic.

Miss Roach
Anyway my friend Pat rang and said that she had finished her seven week rehab and wanted to go clubbing to prove it had worked this time. It was her third time in rehab.

Mr M
Third time lucky then?

Miss Roach
Not really.

Mr M
What happened?

Miss Roach

Well she was fine on the bus and when we walked into the club, she didn't touch a drop.

Mr M

Well she would be, there wasn't a drop to touch.

Miss Roach

Then we found out it was two for one on all drinks.

Mr M

She never had a chance did she?

Miss Roach

No. Especially when she started singing 'I don't want no small dick man' at the bouncers. The hospital has booked her back into rehab. She goes in next Monday. I was professional though.

Mr M

Why was that?

Miss Roach

I went back to this guy's flat and said I would only stay for an hour and I did.

Mr M

So what time did you leave?

Miss Roach

Five.

Mr M

What time did you get up?

Miss Roach

Six.

Mr M

Well we are not going to be getting much from you this morning. Tell me, why you didn't say no when he asked you.

Miss Roach

I was going to, but I found out they call him 'Donkey Dan'. Believe me Mr M, he lives up to his name.

Mr M

This is Mrs Johnson, she has come to give us a hand this morning. Miss Roach is our professional teaching assistant, who looks after Little Jeremy, although as you can see, it's five year old Jeremy who most of the time does the caring for Miss Roach. *(Seeing through the middle window)* Look as though you are busy Miss Roach, the 'head' is approaching. *(Miss Roach pretends she is looking through her planning)*

Miss Bigwood

Good morning everyone.

Mr M

Good morning Miss Bigwood.

Miss Bigwood

Now I hope you are looking after our wonderful Mrs Johnson.

Mo

I'm loving the day already and it's not even nine o'clock yet.

Miss Bigwood

That's wonderful to hear. Whilst I think about it, can you come and see me at dinner time Mr M. I need to know if you can do all next week and maybe next term.

Mr M

Is it for this class?

Miss Bigwood
It is.

Mr M
Is she not well?

Miss Bigwood
Well, you could say that. I'm not one for gossiping.

Mr M
You never have been.

Miss Bigwood
But you know those dating apps she has been on?

Mr M
What, those dating apps she's never had any luck on?

Miss Bigwood
That's the ones. Well Lady Luck seems to have been calling.

Mr M
No!

Miss Bigwood
Well apparently, she met three blokes in one week.

Mr M
Would you believe it.

Miss Bigwood
Now she is pregnant and doesn't know who the father is.

Mr M
Well it's not as though you can trace it back.

Miss Bigwood

But she does know that one of the men has a medical problem, which if he is the father can be transferred to the unborn child.

Mr M

It's like a science fiction movie.

Miss Bigwood

Tell me about it. I keep shouting for Scotty to beam me up. Anyway, I'll see you later. *(As she is walking out she looks at Miss Roach)* Your eyes look a bit bloodshot Miss Roach. In future, when someone phones you up to go out partying, say no on a school night, that way you won't sit there looking at a blank piece of paper. *(She walks out the door)*

Miss Roach

Bitch.

Mr M

Well, you don't do yourself any favours.

Miss Roach

Can't you remember when you were in your twenties?

Mr M

As though it was yesterday. What about you Mrs Johnson?

Mo

With my age, as though it was last week. *(They all laugh)*

Mr M

Right, this morning, I'll do the register, then we will have a chat until assembly.

Miss Roach

Are you going to be talking for an hour?

Mr M

Well, I live on my own with two cats, so I don't get to talk to many people. After assembly, it's playtime. When we come back, we will do a bit of phonics then P.E. Looking at you Miss Roach, you could do with some fresh air. You see Mrs Johnson; I'm always thinking of those around me. *(Miss Roach sticks two fingers up)* Right, let's open the door and let the little darlings in. *(Mr M walks to the door and opens it)* Good morning everyone. What's all these presents I can see? You are all wonderful. *(As the children walk into the classroom)* Pop all the presents onto the table, we will take a look at them in a bit. Coats off children and come and sit on the carpet. Well, here we all are. *(Mr M sits down at the front of the carpet)* Let me get my register and see who we have got this morning. Lucy, good morning.

Lucy

Good morning Mr M.

Mr M

Go and get your present, *(she goes to the table and picks up her present and gives it to Mr M)* Well, what have we got here? *(Mr M opens the present)* A litre bottle of Disaronno. Lucy, how wonderful, give Mr M a hug *(she hugs Mr M)* Let me open your card. *(Mr M opens the card and reads it out loud)* 'Happy birthday Mr M, you are the best teacher ever, love Lucy and a big kiss.' I'm filling up. Lucy, go and get Mr M a tissue. *(This she does)* Now children, would you like to sing Lucy's song? *(the children shout 'yes')* One, two, three.

'Lucy Locket has a hole in her pocket and all three pennies fall through, but Lucy Locket has sown her pocket and now she has pennies for me and you'.

Wasn't that beautiful Mrs Johnson?

Mo

It was Mr M.

Mr M

Can you see children, Lucy has stuck pennies on Mr M's card. Let's count them and see how many there are. *(The children count forty pennies)* Beautiful counting everyone. Thank you lovely Lucy you can have five points. *(She sits down)* James good morning.

James

Good morning Mr M.

Mr M

Would you like to bring over your present? *(James gets a card from the table and gives it to Mr M)* What have we got here? *(Mr M opens the card)* James you wonderful boy. It says 'Happy Birthday Mr M, you are the best' and what is this inside my card? A twenty pound theatre voucher. James how wonderful. Thank you. Five team points to you. Who's next on my register? Gary good morning.

Gary

Good morning Mr M.

Mr M

Would you like to get your present *(he gets the present from the table and gives it to Mr M)* A toilet roll. This is different Gary.

Gary

My mum thought you would like it as she thinks you are full of it.

Mr M

How's you mummy's love life Gary?

Gary

She has not had a sniff for months.

Mr M

Would that be because they can sniff your mummy from ten miles away?

Gary

She often goes to 'Boots'.

Mr M

But does she buy anything when she's there?

Gary

Not yet Mr M.

Mr M

Not ever. Anyway, moving on. Caroline, good morning.

Caroline

Good morning Mr M.

Mr M

Would you like to go and get your present? *(Caroline starts to cry)* Flower, come and see Mr M. Now what's all this?

Caroline

My mummy was supposed to bring it.

Mr M

There's still plenty of time. Wait a minute, whose that at the door?

Caroline

Mummy.

Mr M

Go and let her in. *(Caroline's mum comes into the class)* Hello you wonderful lady. *(Caroline's mum hands over a cake box and a star)* Shall we open it up? *(The children shout yes)* Look at that, it's beautiful, you can't beat a bit of home made. Thank you Miss Love Lace.

Miss Love Lace

You are so worth it Mr M. Are you out tonight?

Mr M

I am. I'm going out with Mr Browny and Mr Woody. What about yourself?

Miss Love Lace

Yeah, I'm out with the girls.

Mr M

I'll see you later then. Did you know Mr Browny is back on the market?

Miss Love Lace

That's good to hear. I'll put my lacy underwear on, they drive men wild.

Mr M

I'll see you later, *(she walks out of the classroom)* what a beautiful cake. *(Caroline sits down)*

Valerie

It's a good job she didn't put candles on it. With so many it would have set the fire alarms off.

Mr M

You have always been a popular girl haven't you Valerie. Jeremy good morning.

Jeremy

Good morning Mr M.

Mr M

Now, before you get my present, take Miss Roach over to the reading corner where she can have a sleep on the cushions. *(Jeremy takes Miss Roach's hand and leads her over to the reading corner. Miss Roach soon falls asleep)* Now Jeremy, what have you brought me? *(Jeremy gives him his present)* A box of continental chocolates, that is wonderful. I will enjoy eating those this weekend. *(Jeremy sits down)* Aegeus, good morning.

Aegeus

(In a low voice) Good morning Mr M.

Mr M

Anything for me?

Aegeus

My mum has drank all the Ouzo.

Mr M

Your dad still not sure if he is Arthur or Martha?

Aegeus

For the last two weeks he has been Martha.

Mr M

Hence the reason there is no Ouzo. Do you know Mrs Johnson, Aegeus is a Greek boy who will one day go into the world and fight for freedom and justice, isn't that right Aegeus?

Aegeus

They won't mess with me when they see my guns.

Mr M

Thank you Aegeus. Moving on, Robert, good morning.

Robert

Good morning Mr M.

Mr M

How's your mum, 'Mystic Meg'?

Robert

She had a punter come round last night. She wanted to get in contact with her late mother.

Mr M

Did she manage it?

Robert

She did. When she got through to her, her mother told the daughter to sod off and said she was in the middle of something that her daughter could only dream of, seeing that no-one would want to touch a twenty-five stone lump of lard. The daughter passed out and mum had to drag her out. As she did so the woman's purse fell out of her pocket.

Mr M

Hence the reason I've got another bottle of Disaronno. Robert, you are a star. Johnny, good morning.

Johnny

Good morning Mr M.

Mr M

Now, what have you brought? *(Johnny passes Mr M his present)* Now what have we got here? Johnny, a bottle of 'Paco Rabanne'. Thank you so much. Do you know, I'm going to put that on tonight when I'm out celebrating. A round of applause for Johnny everyone. Mabel good morning.

Mabel

Good morning Mr M.

Mr M

What is this you have brought me? A C.D. 'The Best of Cliff Richard' That's wonderful. Do you know I bought a ticket to see Cliff Richard and I thought his concert was on the 21st of December, but it was on the 21st of November, so Mr M missed it. That ticket cost me fifty pounds. But I've now got all his songs on my CD, thanks to my Able Mabel. Do you know, Mrs Johnson, Mabel is able to do anything. Not only did she wash my car last week, but she sewed a couple of buttons on my shirt. She even cut my hair. That reminds me, I want you to book me a week in Spain online.

Mabel

Leave it with me.

Mr M

She's wonderful. Zeeta and Rita my beautiful twins good morning.

Zeeta/Rita

Good morning Mr M.

Mr M

Anything for me? *(they both hand over a card each)* What have we got here? *(Opening the cards)* Two ten pounds vouchers for Zara. My favourite shop. Do you know girls, I was going to pop in there this afternoon. I could do with a new tight shirt to show off my muscles. Do you know everyone, I can't believe you have brought me such wonderful presents. I just don't know how you knew what to buy.

Valerie

You have been banging on about your birthday for the last few weeks. In fact, you gave a list out to each child telling them they had to tick off which one they were going to buy.

Mr M

Thank you Valerie. Anything for Mr M?

Valerie

My mum said she would rather stick needles into her eye lids than buy you anything.

Mr M

I'm surprised your mother has got any needles left with her habit. Valerie, would you like to stand up and walk to the door, and when you go through it, close it. *(Valerie does as she is told)* Now my little Amy, good morning.

Amy

Good morning Mr M. *(She gives him her present)*

Mr M

Now what could this be? Wow, a new pair of shoes, and they are a size 9. What a star you are. Everyone give Amy a round of applause *(the children do this)* Amy love, go and show Mrs Johnson your doll. *(Amy goes to her drawer and gets her doll. She takes it to Mo)*

Mo

Thank you.

Mr M

Now Mrs Johnson, as you can see, Amy's doll is pregnant. Now rotate the tummy. *(As she does this, she sees there are two babies in the dolls stomach)*

Mo

Mr M, what can I say?

Mr M

It's amazing in a disturbing sort of way. Amy is obsessed with babies. How old are you Amy?

Amy

Five.

Mr M

When is mummy due?

Amy

Two months, three weeks and two days.

Mr M

Would you like any of your own Amy?

Amy

Enough for a football team.

Mr M

Moving on. David and Marvin good morning.

David/Marvin

Good morning Mr M.

Mr M

Now, Mrs Johnson, these two super boys not only live next door to each other, but they have two mums who cook the most amazing Caribbean food. *(They give Mr M a box. He opens it)* Boys that looks and smells amazing. I'm going to have this jerk chicken with a salad for my tea tonight. Thank you boys. Well thank you everyone for my presents. They have come as a complete surprise to me. Lucy go and get another tissue.

James

How's Kevin the cat?

Mr M

He's very well and so is Gerald the ginger cat.

James

Are they getting on now?

Mr M

Much better, although, they still like to avoid each other.

James

How is Peter puss cat?

Mr M

Well I don't see him a lot, but I always give him a bit of food when I do.

James

Has he still not had his bits chopped off?

Mr M

No. He is still wandering around, hoping to find a lady cat. Mrs Johnson, would you like to hear James' story?

Mo

I would.

Mr M

Go and fetch it flower, *(he fetches his book)* Now, come and stand next to me. Right in a loud voice off you go.

Jeremy

Kevin the cat was feeling grumpy as he walked down the garden path. He saw Gerald the ginger cat and said to him "Don't you think it's time you went on a diet, you fat ginger pig?" Five minutes later he saw Peter puss cat. Kevin said "You need to clean yourself up and have the snip." The end.

Mr M

Wasn't that brilliant, round of applause *(as the children are clapping, Miss Roach can be seen sleep walking, saying "Where is Donkey Dom, I need Donkey Dom" Jeremy, take Miss Roach back to the reading corner. (Jeremy does this)*

Robert

Mr M, how's your trees going?

Mr M

They are doing well thank you Robert. I didn't get many plums, but the pears were wonderful. *(Miss Archer comes into the class)* Talking about wonderful pears, what can I do for you Miss Archer?

Miss Archer

Just to remind you, assembly starts in five minutes.

Mr M

Thank you Miss Archer, we are on our way. *(Miss Archer leaves the classroom)* Now just before we go, lets sing Mrs Johnson our song. One, two, three.

The Children

Gerald the ginger cat, Gerald the ginger cat, Gerald the ginger cat, Gerald the ginger cat, Kevin the cat, Kevin the Cat, Kevin the cat, cat, cat, Peter puss cat, Peter puss cat, we love you for that.

Mr M

Well done everyone, I hope you liked it Mrs Johnson?

Mo

It was wonderful.

Mr M

Right everyone, line up at the door *(the children line up at the door. Mr M opens the door and sees Valerie)* Go and join the back of the line. (Valerie does this) Right, lets see who's ready. Gary, finger out of your nose and Amy stand up straight.

Amy

I can't Mr M, I'm going to have a baby.

Mr M

Amy dear, take that cushion from under your jumper and give it to Mrs Johnson. No wonder I've not got any hair. Right, off we go. *(They walk to the hall and the children sit in a row at the front Mr M sits at the side next to Mo. Mr Browny sits on the other side of Mr M. (Mr M whispers to Mr Browny)* Whose assembly is it?

Mr Browny

Mr Woody's.

Mr M

Not boat building again.

Mr Browny

It looks like it.

Mr Woody

For this assembly I thought we would look at Noah's Ark, and find out how they built it.

Mr Browny

We will never get this time back again.

Mr Woody

Now, I doubt if you know, but I have built a few boats in my time.

Mr M

(*Whispering*) No, I never knew that. (*As Mr Woody is talking, some children start yawning. Mr Browny leans over and whispers*)

Mr Browny

That Woody has lost the plot.

Mr M

I need a fag. Have you brought some?

Mr Browny

I thought it was your turn?

Mr M

Bloody hell. Ask Charlie from year six to meet me at the back of the green-house. He's bound to have some.

Mr Browny

Will do.

Mr M

He's on about what nails they used now.

Mr Browny

Did you hear that James McCallit is leaving.

Mr M

I never liked the bloke. I always thought he was a right tosser.

Mr Browny

That's all he could be, with his ugly looks.

Mr M

Even if the women were pissed, they wouldn't touch him.

Mr Browny
The children in his class knew more going into his class than leaving it.

Mr M
Was that who they were collecting for the other week?

Mr Browny
It was, although I had to take a pound out of the collection tin to pay off Charlie.

Mr M
That's funny, I did the same *(they both laugh)* He's talking about what's the best wood you need to build a boat now.

Mr Browny
Talking of wood, here comes Bigwood.

Mr M
I hear they have to have 12 inch pieces of wood for her to get on board.

Mr Browny
And that's just the top deck. *(They both laugh)*

Mrs Bigwood
Thank you Mr Woody, I'm sure everyone found that interesting. I would have listened to it myself, but I was watching the paint dry in my office. Good morning children.

The Children
Good morning Mrs Bigwood. Good morning everyone.

Mrs Bigwood
Now I know you have been sitting down forever, but I have an announcement to make. First, someone very close to our hearts

has a special birthday today. So after three *(they all sing happy birthday to Mr M)* Come up Mr M, we have a couple of presents for you *(Mr M goes to the front and collects his presents, opening them)*

Mr M

A litre bottle of Disaronno, and a fifty pounds gift voucher. Thank you so much everyone! *(He gives Mrs Bigwood hug)*

Mrs Bigwood

Also Mr McCallit who is sadly leaving us today, after being with us for over five years. Here are some gifts for you, and we wish you all the best in your new life in India. *(Everyone claps)*

Mr Browny

I hear the ladies of the night only ever charge a few rupees for it out there. He might get lucky.

Mr M

I'm not sure, they are bound to charge him double.

As Mr McCallit goes back to his seat, he stops and thanks Mr Browny for his help and support.

Mr Browny

(To James McCallit) We are all going to miss you. *(He goes and sits down.)*

Mr M

Do you know Mr Browny, I don't know which face I'm talking to when I speak to you, I'll see you in five minutes. Right children, stand up and follow me, *(they all go back to the classroom)* Get your snacks and put your coats on, it's very cold outside. *(The children go out)* Valerie and Gary, have you had any breakfast this morning?

Valerie/Gary
No Mr M.

Mr M
I've bought you a couple of breakfast bars. Mrs Johnson, get yourself off to the staffroom for a cuppa, I'm off for a fag.

Mr M walks round to the greenhouse at the side of the school, where Mr Browny is talking to Charlie.

Mr Browny
Have you heard this Mr M?

Mr M
What have I heard?

Mr Browny
Charlie's fags are going up.

Charlie
I'm sorry chaps, but my mum wants to go away for a short break next month.

Mr M
Well, the prices she is charging, she must be spending the weekend in the Caribbean.

Charlie
So you don't want any fags then?

Mr M
Here's two quid. *(Charlie gives Mr M two cigarettes)* Now clear off *(Charlie walks away)*

Mr Browny
Even the kids are on the make.

Mr M

Where are we meeting tonight?

Mr Browny

How about eight o'clock at 'The Laughing Cow'? I hear police-man Mickey is performing.

Mr M

Is Woody still coming?

Mr Browny

He will be there in body.

Mr M

A couple of doubles and he's on his back. No wonder policeman Mickey's mum came out of the toilet with a big smile on her face.

Mr Browny

It doesn't bear thinking about.

Mr M

Right, I'm off to do my phonics.

Mr M walks back to the classroom, where he is met by the children in a line.

Mr M

Right you lot, coats off and sit on the carpet. I thought we would do a bit of phonics for twenty minutes, then a bit of P.E. Now, I know Miss Roach has a group but...

Jeremy

It would be like trying to raise the dead Mr M.

Mr M

In that case, we will do it all together. Now, as you know we have been looking at the first five letters of the alphabet.

Everyone together.

The Children
'A, B, C, D, E'

Mr M
'A' is for? *(The children put their hands up)* Jeremy.

Jeremy
'A' is for alcohol.

Mr M
Why alcohol?

Jeremy
Because Mr M likes to have a double Disaronno on a Friday night, when he is watching 'Gardens World'.

Mr M
Well done. 'B'? *(Hands go up)* Lucy.

Lucy
'B' is for 'beautiful'.

Mr M
Why beautiful?

Lucy
Because Mr M is a beautiful person.

Mr M
Well done. 'C'? *(Hands go up)* Mabel.

Mabel
Carrot cake.

Mr M
Why carrot cake?

Mabel
Because it's one of Mr M's favourite cakes.

Mr M
Well done. 'D'? *(Hands go up)* Johnny.
Johnny
'D' is for 'Dead or alive'.

Mr M
Why 'Dead or alive'?

Johnny
Because you spin me right round, baby, right round like a record player, right round, right round.

Mr M
Well done Johnny. 'E'? *(Hands go up)* Marvin.

Marvin
Eggcellent.

Mr M
Why 'eggcellent'?

Marvin
Because you are an excellent teacher who loves eggs.

Mr M
Well done Marvin. Right, girls go and get your P.E kits. *(The girls go off)*

Robert
What are we doing for P.E?

Mr M

I thought a bit of footie would be good. *(All the boys cheer)* Right, go and get your P.E kits. When you are changed sit on the carpet.

As the children are changing Mr M goes over to Miss Roach in the reading corner.

David

Is Sleeping Beauty still asleep?

Mr M

Sleeping yes, but beauty, you need to go to Specsavers David. *(Everyone laughs)* Miss Roach *(in a quiet voice)* are you awake?

Miss Roach

Is that Donkey Dan?

Mr M

No love, that donkey bolted hours ago. *(In a loud voice)* Now get yourself up. We are going outside for P.E. In future, stick to donkey rides on Skeggy beach. Miss Roach is wide awake children. *(The children all cheer)*

Lucy

Can you do my buttons Mr M?

Mr M

Go and see Miss Roach, she knows how to press a button and, if she carries on, it will be the button of destruction where her job is concerned. Now that we are all on the carpet, line up at the door. *(At the door)* I want you to run down the playground and back again. Then I want you to stand on the yellow line. *(Mr M opens the door and the children run out)* Come on Caroline, I know you can only run to your mother's fridge, but do try. Right, now that you are on the yellow line, those who want to play football, stay on the line. Everyone else, go with Miss Roach, good luck with that. So there's just Aegeus who doesn't want to play football. I hope, Mabel, that now you can see that Aegeus doesn't want to play football it has made up your mind who to choose as a boyfriend. As you can see, Johnny is playing football.

Mabel
It has Mr M *(she shouts)* Aegeus, I want someone who can play a man's game, you're dumped!

Mr M
Now we have sorted Mabel's love life out, we will make a start. Zeeta, you are captain number one. Rita, you are captain number two. *(Each of the girls choose their teams)* Right captains, sort out your teams playing position *(Mr M goes to the middle of the pitch)* Zeeta, you're taking kick off. *(Mr M blows his whistle and they begin)*

Mo
The twins are amazing.

Mr M
That's why I chose them as captains. They both just run the game.

Mo
Do you know Mr M, you are an amazing teacher. I have never seen anything like it. Your teaching methods and the way you have these children in the palm of you hand is incredible.

Mr M
You are too kind Mrs Johnson. Do you know I've been teaching now for about twenty-six years, and in that time I must've taught between a quarter and half a million children. Which I must admit, there is no other teacher who has ever taught as many.

Mo

A truly remarkable legacy to have.

Mr M

I do feel very blessed. Which no-one can take away from me.

Mo

You sound as though it's coming to an end Mr M?

Mr M

Nothing lasts forever, as you know. But as one chapter closes, another one opens. About a year ago, I became an author, which is pretty remarkable knowing what I have been through in my life. My second book should be coming out in the next couple of weeks. Do you know, Mrs Johnson, to see and hear people laughing and enjoying what you have written is truly amazing.

Mo

I bet it is. You must sell me a copy before I go.

Mr M

I've got one for you. That is definitely a foul. *(He runs onto the pitch, picks up the ball and takes it to the penalty spot)*

Rita

Penalty ref, you need your eyes testing Mr M. Have you got money on the other side to win?

Mr M

(Showing Rita the yellow card) Right Zeeta, who is taking the penalty?

Zeeta

Robert Mr M.

Mr M
Are you in goal Johnny? *(Johnny puts his thumb up)* Here we go.

Mr M blows his whistle and Robert shoots and scores. Robert can be seen running around the pitch with his top off. Johnny starts to cry.

Mabel
(To Johnny) I don't want a wimp as a boyfriend. You're dumped!

Mr M
(Mr M blows his whistle) Right everyone. Get to the classroom and get dressed. Let's see who will be the first ready for dinner. *(In the classroom)* Did you have a nice time with Miss Roach, Aegeus?

Aegeus
I only saw her for five minutes. She had to go to the toilet and I didn't see her after that.

Mr M
You were lucky to see her for five minutes.

Miss Roach
When you have got to go, you have got to go.

Mr M
I see the vodka is still leaking out of you, with the whiskey chasing it. *(To the children on the carpet)* I've had a wonderful morning, and your morning, Mrs Johnson?

Mo
I will never forget it.

Mr M
I hope you don't. Come and see us again soon.

Mo

I will.

Mr M

Right children. Line up for the dinner lady. *(The children all line up for the dinner lady. Mr M goes to the front of the line)* Morning Mrs Cartwright.

Mrs Cartwright

Morning Mr M.

Mr M

How's your Bert's back?

Mrs Cartwright

He tried to get his leg over last night.

Mr M

Did he succeed?

Mrs Cartwright

No, he got stuck half way over. It took hours to get his leg back again. I missed my programme.

Mr M

What was that?

Mrs Cartwright

'Naked Attraction' I like to look at the tattoos.

Mr M

Follow Mrs Cartwright everyone *(she leads the children out)* Thank you Mrs Johnson.

Mo

It's been a pleasure.

Mr M

Miss Roach, give me a hug, I need to sniff the alcohol fumes coming off you, it'll get me ready for tonight.

Miss Roach

I need the toilet again. *(She rushes out of the classroom)*

Mr M

Right, I'd better go and see what the head wants. Thank you again Mrs Johnson.

Mo

It will be a great loss to the teaching profession when you leave.

Mr M

You are a star. Come and see us again soon. *(Mr M walks out of the classroom)*

Mo puts on her coat, and whilst waving to Billy in the dining hall, she walks to the car park where Ron is waiting for her.

Ron

Did you have a good morning?

Mo

It was incredible.

I Only Came In For A Haircut

Characters
Mo, Phoebe, Janice, Vera Virus, Carol and Frigging Freda.

Setting
The Blow and Go (hairdressers).

I Only Came In For A Haircut

Mo walks into the hairdressers eating an apple where she is confronted by everyone.

Vera Virus

Here comes the teacher's pet. An apple for the teacher.

Mo

You lot get worse. I'll have you know I was a good girl.

Vera Virus

You've changed.

Phoebe

How did you get on love?

Mo

Do you know I had a great morning. The children were wonderful and Mr M was incredible. If he had been my teacher back in the day, I'd have been the Prime Minister by now. He is so inspirational.

Vera Virus

Can you imagine her as Prime Minister? Everyone would be alcoholics. She would tell her Chancellor of the Exchequer to get rid of the tax on beer and spirits. Also, she would make sure everyone was into free love and tell them to leave their bedroom windows open.

Mo

(laughing) Vera, however your Bert puts up with you, I will never know.

Vera Virus

He puts up with me because I keep his bush nice and trimmed. *(They laugh)* Don't you think it's time you had a colour on your hair? Grey doesn't help to conceal your age very well. You might play the part of a Grandma well, but you don't want to look the part, especially in the bedroom.

Mo

Thank you for that Vera, you need to get a job at the Samaritans - you would kill half of the population.

Phoebe

Vera has got a point. With a new husband you do need him to rise on every occasion when he looks into your eyes. Let's be honest, a man of a certain age, could easily have his shares in Viagra.

Mo

Well, you really know how to make a girl feel good about herself. Have you got any rope? I'll go and find the nearest tree.

Vera Virus

Don't use that tree in the square, the branches wouldn't take your weight.

Mo

I'm going to slap you two in a minute.

Phoebe

Talking of trees, I'm light as a chestnut. Although Vera, do you think it would be dark enough to cover all of the grey?

Vera Virus

(They have both got their fingers in Mo's hair) Mind you, talking of trees, I think we would have to go darker with the roots.

Janice comes into the hairdressers.

Phoebe

Morning Janice love. We were just thinking what the best colour would be for Mo's snowstorm disaster.

Janice

(Walking over, she puts her fingers into Mo's hair) What colour did you say?

Phoebe

I thought a light chestnut.

Janice

Not with the colour of those roots. You would have to go darker.

Carol comes into the hairdressers

Carol

Hiya girls. What's happening here?

Phoebe

We were trying to get the right colour for Mo's hair. I thought a light chestnut.

Carol

(Putting her fingers in Mo's hair) Not with those roots. It also depends on the length she has it.

Phoebe

You have got a point.

Mo

Does anyone know why I'm here?

Vera Virus

I thought about a fringe, so it keeps the hair off her face.

Phoebe

I can see what you are saying, but it would reveal her lines.

Carol

Those lines do resemble Paddington train station.

Vera Virus

We will have to keep the length. That way it would save her fifty quid on having her eyebrows done.

Mo

Have you finished?

Vera Virus

We will have to take a vote *(Mo has her mouth open)* Hands up for light chestnut? That's no-one. Hands up for just chestnut *(two hands go up)* and hands up for dark chestnut *(two hands go up)* That's a tie.

Carol

Tell you what, we will have to toss a coin.

Mo

This is my hair we are talking about.

Carol

I've got a coin, heads for just chestnut, tails for dark chestnut.

Phoebe

That's fair.

Mo

Well, it's not everyday you get your hair style by the toss of a coin.

Carol

(Throwing the coin. It comes down heads) Just chestnut it is.

Mo

Well, I'm glad we have decided on the toss of a coin. It's a good job Bella isn't here otherwise it would've taken another hour to decide.

Vera Virus

Have you not heard?

Everyone

What?

Vera Virus

Bella has now got a new boyfriend.

Phoebe

Really? Who is it?

Vera Virus

You will never guess.

Carol

Who?

Vera Virus

Policeman Mickey.

Phoebe

No, I can't believe it.

Carol

How did this happen?

Vera Virus

Well, apparently they found themselves in the same clothes shop.

Carol

Which one?

Vera Virus

That clothes shop in the high street.

Carol

You mean 'Tight is Right'?

Vera Virus

That's the one. Mind you, the owner is as tight as they come. There was this woman who had fallen in love with one of her dresses. When she went to pay, she found that she was a pound short. Would that tight bitch let her off a pound? Not a chance. Anyway, the woman, who was heartbroken, left the shop to see if she knew anybody who could lend her a pound. He said, "of course I can, but you will have to do something for me first". The next minute, the woman found herself in an ally, giving the man oral sex.

Janice

She didn't?

Vera Virus

She did. That's what the love of a dress did to her. Anyway, the man she went with happened to be a neighbour of hers.

Janice

No.

Vera Virus

He was, and to cut a long story short, her husband found out and threw her out. You can now see her most nights wearing the dress, on Prostitutes Way. Anyway, back to the story. Bella, as you knew always wears tight fitting dresses that go to her knees. That way she doesn't have to wear any underwear. Anyway, earlier she got talking to a bloke online who wanted to take her for a Chinese.

Carol

Well, she does love her chicken balls.

Vera Virus

The guy was only twenty-one.

Phoebe

Lucky bitch.

Vera Virus

This twenty-one year old, had a fetish for lace underwear, so Bella had to find a dress that was short enough to show her lace knickers off. Trying this dress on, she slipped and fell, ripping the back of the dress. This revealed her bottom. Well, who do you think was in the next cubicle, trying on and off the shoulder number to sing 'The Bitch'.

Mo

Policeman Mickey.

Vera Virus

Correct. Hearing the crash, Policeman Mickey looked over the top of the cubicle and saw Bella on the floor with her bottom on show for the whole world to see. It was like a magnet to policeman Mickey. He climbed over the cubicle, picked Bella up and kissed her. She has had chicken balls every night this week.

Phoebe

I'm lucky to get a spring roll.*(They all laugh)*

All of a sudden, Frigging Freda bursts through the door.

Vera Virus

Bloody hell girl, are your knickers on fire?

Frigging Freda
Have you not heard?

Mo
Heard what?

Frigging Freda
Sarah Summers has died.

Carol
Never, not Sarah Summers.

Mo
How did she die?

Frigging Freda
Well, according to Zit Faced Zita, do you know I gave her a letter I was sending to my sister in Norway. A I passed it over, some of her pus from her zits fell onto my letter.

Carol
Dirty cow.

Frigging Freda
Do you know what she said?

Phoebe
What?

Frigging Freda
She said, with their snowy weather, it makes the letter more authentic.

Vera Virus
Disgusting. They need to stick a health warning on her face.

Mo

Well, how did she die?

Frigging Freda

Oh yes, well, Zit Faced Zita said, it was around four yesterday afternoon, that Sarah decided to have afternoon tea. One of her slaves, who just finished cleaning the grates out with his underpants, was told to fetch some tea, with a slice of chocolate cake. The slave brings what he is told and as Sarah is just about to take a bite of the cake, she says to the slave "you did wash your hands didn't you?" the slave said "no". Sarah went ballistic. She rubbed the cake all over his face and dragged him by his hair to the whipping wall. She caned him once, then said 'the next one is going to hurt me more than it will you'. So as she lifted her arm to cane him again, she developed chest pains, as she had over-stretched herself. She collapsed on the floor. Now, if an ambulance had been called straight away, they could've saved her, but the stroke had left her slurring her words, so she couldn't give any clear instructions to her slaves as to what to do. She died twenty minutes later. She was found two hours later, with the slaves walking around like the 'Stepford wives' waiting for new instructions.

Janice

That's shocking.

Phoebe

Well, she was right, when she said it's going to hurt me more than it's going to hurt you.

Mo

Do we know when the funeral is going to be?

Frigging Freda

Well, zit faced Zita thinks in a couple of weeks, but there is a will reading first. So anyone could get a letter to attend next week.

Vera Virus
Well, this will be the second funeral this year, and it's not even Easter yet.

Carol
That's the trouble with getting older; you go to more funerals than weddings. Mind you, if my husband doesn't pull his finger out, we will be going to another funeral. Do you know what he said to me the other day?

Mo
What?

Carol
He said he wanted to do some charity work. I told him "charity begins at home" so I told him to get himself up them stairs and sort out the spare room. He said "That's my den, which has got all my personal possessions in". I told him, "that's my spare room, that has got your junk in it." I said you have been watching too much Dragons Den. We will see how much money that junk is worth when we take it down to the car boot. I told him then, it's time to get rid, this dragon has spoken. He didn't speak to me for hours after that. It was the first time I could watch my soaps without his gob going.

Vera Virus
(Swivelling round Mo's chair) What do you think girls?

Everyone goes over to look at Mo's hair.

Janice
It definitely takes ten years off of you.

Phoebe
That might be a bit ambitious.

Mo

You cheeky cow.

Carol

Let's have a look at your roots. *(They all put their fingers in Mo's hair)* It's got rid of all that grey. All you need to do now is to dye your lower bits to match.

Mo

Thank you Carol.

Phoebe

I think with this new look, she won't be swinging from the tree, she will be swinging from her bedroom chandelier.

Frigging Freda

I hope it is reinforced.

Mo

(Standing up) Right you witches, I'm going. I'll see you in a couple of weeks for the funeral.

She kisses each one and walks out of the hairdressers and down the street.

Self Reflection

The Will In The Morning, The Funeral In The Afternoon

Characters

Paul Sweet

A young, good looking solicitor, who is around six foot tall.

Phil and Philomema

A small couple who have been married for over seventy years. They know Mo from her childhood.

Other Characters

Mo, Phoebe, Carol, Vera Virus, Harold and pissed up Pete who likes it neat.

Setting

The solicitors office, the church.

The Will in the Morning, the Funeral in the Afternoon

Mo is seen walking into the solicitor's after going to the reception, she is led into the small office of Paul Sweet.

Paul

Good morning Mrs Johnson.

Mo

Good morning Mr Sweet.

Paul

Do take a seat. I'm sure you are acquainted with Miss Dickson and Mrs Bloomer.

Mo

Vaguely, Mr Sweet. I hear they don't have the best reputations.

Phoebe

Are you going to slap her or am I?

Paul

Thank you Miss Dickson. Please control yourself. *(Mo is seen laughing)*

Harold comes through the door

Harold

Good morning.

Paul

Good morning Mr Hardcastle.

Harold

It's Mr Castle. I've not been hard for many years.

Phoebe

Well, that's a surprise.

Carol

With his weight, you would never know.

Harold

What do you mean? What are you saying? What are you implying?

Paul

My apologies Mr Castle. I don't know how that mistake could happen.

Phoebe

It amazes us too.

Harold

What do you mean? What are you... *(the door opens and stops Harold from saying any more)*

Vera Virus enters the room.

Vera Virus

I'm sorry I'm late but the new girl, Ann, got the dyes mixed up. I've never seen so many pinks and greens. One old dear said, "I've never had this much green in my hair since I went rolling in the grass with my husband and his male lover."

Carol

No.

Vera Virus

Best thing was she felt like a carrot and cucumber sandwich.

Phoebe

Well, it was certainly the right filling for her. How old is she?

Vera Virus

Ninety-two.

Phoebe

She must have a good memory?

Vera Virus

It was a special treat for her ninetieth birthday.

Phoebe

Bloody hell, if she continues like that she will be under the grass not on top of it.

Paul

Thank you Mrs Winter-Bottom. Now that we are all here, I think it is time we begin. *(He opens the will)* Now, looking through the will, I can honestly say it's not one that I have ever seen before and I'm sure I will never see one like it again. The will stipulates that the half a million pounds, that Miss Summers has accumulated, will be put into a trust in order to keep her slaves happy and secure. She proposes that her house and dungeon is made into a museum.

Carol

I'm hearing this right?

Paul

You are.

Phoebe

Well, I don't see what we have to do with it?

Paul

Let me continue Miss Dickson, all will be revealed. Now, in order for her business to continue, Miss Summers wants a committee to be set up, that can look after every section of her business. That includes the house, dungeon, the cleaning contracts with the bus company and with the private houses. Miss Summers also states that twice a day visitors from the general public can be given tours of the house and dungeon, so they can see the valuable work being done within the community.

Phoebe

I don't think I can be part of this. I have my good name and reputation to think about.

Mo

That should take you all of five seconds.

Phoebe

I don't know what you mean.

Paul

Thank you Miss Dickson. If you could just bear with me for a little longer.

Harold

(Whispering to Mo) For him I could bear all. Sweet by name, sweet by nature. I could wrap him in sweetie paper, all over his naked body.

Paul

Did you say something Mr Castle?

Harold

Not a word Mr Sweet.

Paul

In that case, I will continue. Now, Miss Summers stipulates that in order for the museum to be profitable, you will need to employ at least three people to see to the daily running of things. Firstly, you will need to employ someone to look after the catering side of things. I propose Mini Meg and now that Penny scrubs her hands each time she cooks, 'the dirty bitch', I suggest that Penny helps her as long as she keeps those plasters on. Miss Summers also suggests that there should be a tour guide. She proposes, someone like Mrs Bloomer for the job. Miss Summers believes what Mrs Bloomer has up top and dressed in a dominatrix outfit will make the place look more authentic to the visitors.

Carol

I could do that.

Paul

Finally, Miss Summers states that a dominatrix needs to be employed, to give two half-hour shows. As a committee, she suggest you hold auditions. Miss Summers has left a list of possible candidates. Now, Miss Summers states the reasons why she has selected you fine people to become committee members. She states that Mr Castle should become the chairman. Miss Summers states now that Herbert has left to go in search of ladyboys in Thailand, and with Mary at university, being chairman will get you off your lard ass and give you something to do, rather than watching porn all day, stuffing your fat face with popcorn.

Harold

Cheeky bitch.

Paul

Miss Summers proposes that you, Mrs Johnson, becomes the

treasurer. She states that not only you are the most honest woman she has ever met, but also one of the most hard working women she has met. She says that although you spend eighty percent of your day in the bedroom, she knows the accounts will get done.

Phoebe
Is it only eighty percent? I thought it was more.

Mo
I don't know what you mean. *(They all laugh)*

Paul
As for Mrs Bloomer, it would be good to have a working committee member. Someone who could report back to the committee on the day to day running of things. Miss Summers does say, that this might be the first job you are very good at.

Carol
Nasty witch.

Paul
As for Mrs Winter-Bottom, Miss Summers states that, for good business to succeed, it needs to be advertised. So I propose that you become the museums PR agent, with the size of your gob it should flourish.

Vera Virus
Nasty cow.

Paul
Lastly, Miss Summers says 'why oh why would I want Phoebe Dickson on my committee, I'm sure has left you scratching you heads. *(Everyone on the room is scratching their heads)*

Phoebe
You vile lot.

Paul

However, like Mo, you say how it is and apart from sex, you never let anything get the better of you. Now, we all know your tartish nature, *(everyone nods their heads)* but you are a tart with a heart and that's why I want you to take Ben Hung under your wing, so you can take care of his more sensitive side. Although he will need a kick up the bum from time to time.

Mo

It's a shame you won't be able to help and look after Ben. You of course will want to keep your good name and reputation.

Phoebe

I know what you are saying, but I would be helping a dear friend. A friend who with her last dying breath had thought of Ben and said my name. When people find out, they will likely see me as a hero.

Mo

So the fact that Ben is hung like a donkey, your vibrator is broken and you hate cleaning, has nothing to do with you back tracking.

Phoebe

It's not as though I am back tracking, its just the fact that I want to fulfil the last dying wish of a friend.

Everyone

Tart.

Harold

Well, if that's all Mr Sweet?

Paul

Yes, that concludes the reading. I would just like to say however, that Miss Summers has a mix of clientèle, from all walks of life.

So the law is very much behind what you are doing. Now that you have all agreed to Miss Summers proposals, there is an envelope that I must give each of you. Thank you for coming.

Harold
Thank you Mr Sweet.

As each member of the committee gets up, they collect their envelope and leave the room. As they get outside, they discover each envelope has a cheque in it for five thousand pounds.

Mo
Well, talk about life giving you the unexpected.

Harold
In this village, there's never a dull moment. Right, the funeral is in a couple of hours, so I'll see you at the church. *(They all walk off in the direction of their homes)*

A couple of hours later Mo, Phoebe, Harold and Carol are standing outside the church. Vera Virus comes running up the church path.

Vera Virus
Hi everyone, sorry I'm late, but Bella is having a meltdown.

Mo
What happened?

Vera Virus
Bella got the new girl to dye her hair.

Phoebe
What colour?

Vera Virus

Cream. She thought it would remind Policeman Mickey of last weekend when they brought cream into their sex life.

Carol

How does that work?

Vera Virus

Well, you know how Wimbledon is famous for strawberries and cream, and seeing as they both love tennis they wanted to recreate the tastes of Wimbledon. So, Policeman Mickey dipped the strawberries into the cream and placed them on Bella's breasts. Bella said to him, "How many strawberries have you used?" and he said "Fifteen love." Then Bella started feeding Policeman Mickey strawberries. He said, "How many have I had?" Bella said "Thirty love."

Phoebe

This is so erotic.

Vera Virus

Wait for it. Then Bella said "Next time, let's use raspberries, that way you can get more in." He said "How many do you think?" She said, "Forty love."

Mo

This gets worse.

Vera Virus

When they had finished having orgasmic sex, Policeman Mickey turned to Bella and said "Game, set and matched." *(They all burst out laughing)* Anyway where was I? Oh yes, so the girl Ann started to mix up the hair dye, when a couple of drops of blood, from her finger goes into the dye.

Carol
Did she cut herself?

Vera Virus
She cut it trying to pull her zip up on her jeans. If she had brought a size eighteen instead of a fourteen, she wouldn't have cut herself. But you know what the young are like, they never want to admit they are overweight. So she puts the dye on and a hour later, the hair has gone bright pink. In tears, Bella turns to me and says "I'm not having him lick candyfloss off my breasts."

Phoebe
Bless her. Well, she will have to stop doing Wimbledon and do McDonald's instead. You can get a pink coloured milkshake from there. Although, a cheeseburger doesn't quite give you the same sexual stimulation.

Mo
Moving on.

Harold
By the looks of it, it's a good job we turned up. Apart from a few slaves, who are washing down the front of the church in backless trousers, there's no-one else here.

Phoebe
I heard she made them cut out the backs of their trousers, so when she kicked them up the bum it left a red mark. That way she could remember who she had kicked.

Vera Virus
I will give her her due. She was always very fair to her slaves. She made sure each one got their money's worth.

Everyone
She did.

Mo

My goodness, I've not seen those two for years.

Phil and Philomena are walking up the church path. Phil is walking like Dick van Dyke when he played the bank owner in Mary Poppins'

Philomena

Hello my darling *(they have a long embrace)* Do you know, the older you get the younger you look.

Harold

(Whispering) I see her eye sight is going.

Phil

Who is it?

Philomena

It's our Mo. Do you remember when we used to babysit for her and her sisters?

Phil

My goodness me, little Maureen. Didn't she lose her virginity at our place?

Philomena

She did. She brought that boy back with her and because he had brought her a bag of chips, she thought he was the one.

Harold

She'd been known to do it for less.

Philomena

The noise coming from the bedroom, we had to turn up the volume of the wireless so we could hear what Tommy Tinder was saying.

Phoebe

She is still as vocal today. Ask the neighbours.

Philomena

No wonder you always had a sore throat.

Mo

What brings you here today?

Philomena

We have come to pay our respects, as Miss Summers was able to help us out a few years ago.

Mo

How was that?

Philomena

Well, we always had a good sex life together, but about ten years ago, Phil went limp just as he was going to take me from the back. Well, we tried everything, role play, S&M, even a threesome, but nothing moved it skywards. So I took him to see Miss Summers. Half a hour later, it was reaching the stars again.

Mo

What did she do?

Philomena

She used a strap-on, and after a good pounding, life was restored. So now I use one every time. It's made him go bow-legged, but it keeps a smile on his face. Hopefully see you later. *(They walk into the church)*

Phoebe

That gives hope to us all. How old is he?

Mo

He got a birthday card from the Queen last year.

Carol

Here comes the coffin.

As the coffin is brought into the church, the pallbearers are having to fight it off the slaves who are trying to get into the coffin. Putting down the coffin at the front of the church, the pallbearers can be seen dragging the slaves out of the church. 'Pissed up Pete, who likes it neat' goes into the pulpit.

Mo

Is he still on the wagon?

Phoebe

No, one of the wheels fell off last week.

Mo

How come?

Phoebe

He did a baptism last week and mistakenly put wine in the font, instead of water. The smell of the wine was too much, so when he was baptising the child, he was saying 'one for you and one for me, one for you and two for me. When the mother lifted the baby out, Pissed up Pete could be seen with his head in the font sucking up the wine. As the family ran out, Pissed up Pete could be seen running after them, trying to lick the baby's forehead.

Mo

Shocking.

Pissed up Pete

Well, you don't see that every day. Anyone would think we were at a football match. *(Pissed up Pete starts to sing)* 'It's coming home, it's coming home, football's coming home'.

Phoebe
I wish someone would kick his balls.

A noise can be heard coming from the coffin.

Carol
Bloody hell, it's like watching a horror movie.

Pissed up Pete
And who are you Mrs Bloomer, 'The Bride of Dracula?'

Carol
If I was sucking your neck, I would be drinking blood that was a hundred percent proof.

The pallbearers lift off the coffin lid, and discover one of the slaves inside.

Vera Virus
I didn't know they had a buy one get one free offer on.

The pallbearers take him outside.

Harold
We need to get a dominatrix as soon as possible. The slaves need leadership.

Pissed up Pete
(Swaying) What can I say about Sarah Summers? Nothing really. She didn't really have any friends. Made her money from immoral means and beat the crap out of those men she surrounded herself with. What more is there to say.

Mo

Thank you Vicar. As the off licence has just opened, I'm sure you need to be somewhere else.

Pissed up Pete

I do need to get the communion wine *(he passes the church keys to Mo and runs off out of the church. From the pulpit, Mo begins to talk)*

Mo

Unlike some, I can say a lot about Sarah Summers. But before I do, pallbearers, let Sarah's slaves come in. *(The doors are opened and the slaves come down the aisle. Vera has a whip in her hand, she cracks the whip and shouts)*

Vera Virus

Sit. *(The slaves all sit on the floor)*

Mo

I agree that Sarah wasn't the most popular person, in fact even at school the girls hated her. Although that may be because with Sarah's hold over all the boys, it was the first year group where every girl that left was a virgin. Although it didn't take them long to catch up, did it Phoebe?

Everyone

(Nodding their heads) No.

Phoebe

What do you think I am?

Everyone

Tart.

Mo

I know for a fact, if it wasn't for the wives, this church would be packed today. Sarah never discriminated and because of this she helped all sorts of men. Whether they were rich or poor, fat or thin, well endowned or just a maggot. For Sarah, it wasn't about judging someone, but about helping someone. There are not many people who can say that. She made people feel a part of something and gave them a purpose in life. Let's be honest ladies, there are many men out there, who with a good kick up the bum, were able to perform their tasks more effectively and Carol is living proof of that. *(Everyone nods)* But for all of Sarah's faults, she gave so much to the men in her community. With her home becoming a museum, I can announce today the 'Sarah Summer's Foundation' will be set up in order to train new dominatrices, so that the communities around the world can benefit from the work started by Sarah Summers. *(Everyone stands up and claps)*

The Post Office Heist

Characters

Donkey Dick Dave
A small, well hung guy in his mid-thirties

Filthy Phil
Small man in this early forties. He never washes so always smells. He is lacking in education.

Chief Superintendent
A tall dark man in his mid-fifties.

Deb Slapper
A medium height woman in her early thirties. She has six children, all with different fathers. She is around twenty-stone with dyed hair and heavily tattooed.

Other Characters
Mo, Phoebe, Carol, Frigging Freda, Janice, Policeman Mickey, The fella Bella and Zit faced Zita.

Setting
Outside the Post Office.

Self Reflection

The Post Office Heist

Mo, Phoebe and Janice are walking down the high street on their way to having lunch at Ricardo's

Mo

Well, look at us, we have become ladies that lunch.

Phoebe

It is the life I was born for.

Mo

Amongst others.

Phoebe

What's that supposed to mean?

Mo

It means you were born to bring love, affection and happiness to so many.

Phoebe

Are you taking the piss?

Mo

Yes. Talking of happiness, how are you and Ben getting on?

Phoebe

Do you know Mo, its working out wonderfully. He brings me a cup of tea in the morning with just his apron on and as I slap his bottom, he goes off with a smile to do his daily jobs. Do you know Mo, not only can I see out of my windows, but the iron doesn't leave any black marks on my underwear any more.

Mo

I didn't think you wore anything underneath?

Phoebe

I don't usually, but it seems to arouse my Ben. I open the door and with my foot on his naked bottom, I push him out into the garden and tell him to get weeding. You can see the net curtains twitching from the neighbours as they must be thinking why does she have all the luck.

Janice

But it's been freezing of late.

Phoebe

It makes him do the weeding quicker. It also reduces his bits to a manageable size. The vibrator was only six inches.

Janice

He will be carrying you from room to room soon.

Phoebe

I'm on his back twenty-four seven - treat them mean, keep them keen. Although I'm thinking of moving him from the shed into the bathroom. Just in case I want a snack in the night.

Mo

What, a beef sandwich?

Phoebe

I don't know what you mean. *(They all laugh)*

Janice

So where is he now?

Phoebe

He's doing my shift in the shop.

Mo

Do you do anything?

Phoebe

I have lunch with my dear friends. *(They all laugh)*

As they turn the corner, they can see a large crowd gathered outside the Post Office.

Janice

What's happening here?

They walk over to Carol who is standing with Frigging Freda.

Mo

Hi girls, is Hollywood paying us a visit?

Frigging Freda

I wish, getting down and dirty with Jason Statham, now there's a thought.

Mo

So what's going on?

Frigging Freda

Well, about an hour ago, just as Zit Faced Zita was paying Mrs Pointer's pension...

Phoebe

I've not seen her for years. Is she still doing those naked life portraits?

Frigging Freda

Well she was, but as she was painting this young man, she had the television on in the background, which was showing the life story of elephants. She got so engrossed in the programme that when she drew the man's penis, she drew it as a trunk.

Phoebe
That's not good.

Frigging Freda
Well, it got around and now everyone's throwing peanuts at him and tells him to pick them up with his trunk.

Phoebe
Poor sod.

Frigging Freda
So with his confidence at rock bottom, Windy Wendy has taken him under her wing and set him on at her place, so as to help his confidence around men again.

Phoebe
That's kind of her. Has she still got the brothel on Whore's Road?

Frigging Freda
She is still there. I've heard she is raking it in, although she could do with raking her ass.

Phoebe
Is she still?

Frigging Freda
Let's just say the gas that comes out of her could heat every house for a week.

Phoebe
The dirty bitch.

Mo
Mrs Pointer's pension?

Frigging Freda

Oh yes. Well, just as Zit Faced Zita had finished with Mrs Pointer, two men with dark glasses on burst into the Post Office and demanded money. Mrs Pointer told them "You can keep your grubby fingers off my money, especially with those dirty fingernails." She hit him with her handbag and walked out. The robber was dazed, but worse was to come.

Mo

What?

Frigging Freda

When he pointed his gun at Zit Faced Zita, the fear she experienced popped all her zits. So with pus running down her face, the robber passed out. The other robber said "Bloody hell love, have you ever heard of Clearasil?" As he went to help his mate, Zit Faced Zita pressed the alarm button under the counter, and ten minutes later, armed police, the lot, turned up.

Carol

Do you know girls, we all need to get a knife each and run around the streets threatening people. Then when hundreds of police come we can say "We are now getting our money's worth" when we pay our council tax.

Mo

Moving on. Do we know who the two robbers are?

Frigging Freda

Well, when Mrs Pointer remarked how dirty the robber's fingernails were, she suddenly twigged it, it could only be one person.

Mo

Filthy Phil.

Frigging Freda

That's right. Also, when the other robber ran into the Post Office, her eyes were drawn to the larger movement down below. She said it was like Linford Christie running the one hundred metres.

Mo

Donkey Dick Dave.

Frigging Freda

Mrs Pointer said that she drew him once but couldn't get it all in. She had to get a bigger canvas. When she had finished, she charged him double.

Mo

But they were never the brightest pair. There was that time they robbed a jewellers and wore everything they nicked. I think they got a few years for that.

Carol

How about when they robbed a security van and hid all the money in the wheelie bin. The trouble was the bins were collected the next day.

Frigging Freda

The best one is when they tried to rob 'Dirty Kath's Cafe.' They ended up in hospital three days with malaria. *(They all laugh)*

Janice

I see the reporters have arrived. He looks tasty behind the camera.

Mo

I don't think that camera photographs nudes. *(They all laugh)*

Phoebe

Look who they are interviewing.

Janice
Who?

Phoebe
'Dirty Deb, any man in bed.'

Mo
That's not a pretty sight.

Phoebe
Telling me.

Mo
Did you hear that she won a lot of money on the lottery a few months ago? The reporter who interviewed her asked her what's the first think she was going to buy. The reporter said "is it a new home or a new car, or a holiday?" Deb told her it was none of them, and said that she had just been down the offie and brought a crate of lager and a bottle of Baileys for the kids. The six kids with six different fathers.

Phoebe
For some, it doesn't matter how much money they have. It never brings them class.

Mo
Telling me. How long has she had those leggings on, it must be weeks, and as for that t-shirt, that it too tight. It has more stains on it than a whore's knickers.

Janice
Look, the reporter is going to interview her. This will be interesting.

Reporter
Mrs Slappy.

Deb

Miss, never been married love, call me Deb. Everyone else does.

Phoebe

To your face, but behind her back, scrounging slapper comes to mind. *(Everyone laughs)*

Reporter

Are we right in thinking that you know these two robbers?

Deb

Well, sort of. I've only met them once.

Reporter

But aren't they the fathers to your children?

Deb

Just the first two.

Reporter

You have only met them the once?

Deb

It only takes the once to get up the duff, love.

Reporter

What sort of men were they when you met them?

Deb

Haven't got a frigging clue. That's lager for you. Mind you, I did remember a couple of things.

Reporter

What was that?

Deb

Well, when Dave was on top of me, it was like a bus driving into my tunnel.

Reporter

(Shocked) And the other thing?

Deb

With Phil, the bedroom stank that bad, I had to get the council to get me a new bed.

Reporter

Thank you for taking the time to talk to us.

Deb

(Spotting Mo) Hiya Mo, you alright love?

Mo

I'm good thanks Deb.

Deb

Next time you are round my way, pop in, we will have a couple of cans together.

Mo

I'll look forward to it.

Phoebe

I can see you have brought both faces out with you today. *(Everyone in the crowd looks ta Mo and shakes their head)*

Mo

I don't know what you mean. *(They all laugh)*

Carol

Do you know, I'm looking around and there is a group of women sitting down, doing their sewing. There's Frying Fred delivering fish and chip orders. Winkle man Willy is selling his cockles and whelks and the landlord of the 'Flying Cow' has set up an outside bar. It's like a day out at a public hanging.

Phoebe

Well, I can't see us getting to 'Ricardos' now, we better put our order in. Talking about the 'Flying Cow' I have just spotted Marg the Large. There won't be any food left when she gets started.

Mo

Didn't I hear that she went to Spain, and when she was lying down in the swimming pool the birds made nests on top of her, thinking they had reached Australia?

Phoebe

Well, she is as big as an island.

Carol

Hold on, what's happening?

Filthy Phil comes out of the Post Office (everyone holds their nose) and hands over a list of demands to a police officer. The police officer hands the list over to the chief superintendent . The chief superintendent reads out the robbers list, unaware that his megaphone is still on.

Chief Superintendent

(To his officers) He wants a fast car, some food from 'Dirty Kath's Cafe', and some Clearasil. *(Everyone starts to laugh)*

Phoebe

Bloody hell, if he wants food from 'Dirty Kath's Cafe' he must have a death wish.

Frigging Freda
As for the Clearsil, they only have to look at Zita's face for a couple of hours. We all have had to looks at it for years.

Carol
Well, it's taken a robbery for something to be done about it. *(Everyone cheers and starts to celebrate)*

Phoebe
Raise your glass everyone 'To the end of Zita's spots *(everyone repeats it)*

Janice
Isn't that Policeman Mickey over there?

Mo
It is. Everyone waves. *(The crowd waves at Policeman Mickey as Mickey blows them all a kiss)*

Phoebe
I bet Bella doesn't know what's going on?

Carol
I bet she is up to her eyes in perms.

Phoebe
Not any more, I've just text Vera.

Two minutes later, the Fella Bella comes running down the street screaming. She runs past the police cordon and screams Policeman Mickey's name.

Policeman Mickey
(Shouting) Not now babe, can't you see I'm working?

The Fella Bella

I need you. If they kill you, who will I get to lick strawberries and cream off my breasts?

Carol

Me and Tony tried that once with apples and pears.

Mo

Did it work?

Carol

Not really, he left them in the tin. *(They laugh)*

Policeman Mickey

I'm working love.

The Fella Bella

I'm not bothered. You said I was the most important thing in your life. Hold me Mickey, hold me.

Policeman Mickey

(to the Chief Superintendent) Sorry sir, but I'm going to have to sort her out.

Chief Superintendent

You're in the middle of a robbery officer. There are two masked gun men with a hostage.

Policeman Mickey

I know what you are saying sir, but I'll just pop over to comfort her.

Policeman Mickey walks over to the Fella Bella and puts his arms around her.

The Fella Bella
I couldn't bear to lose you.

Policeman Mickey
But you know, I am what I am.

He starts to sing Shirley Bassey's 'I Am What I Am'. He turns to face the crowd as he is singing. The crowd are moving their bodies to the song. When he finishes, the crowd shouts for more. Policeman Mickey sings 'Hey Jude' with the crowd singing along. At the end of the song, Policeman Mickey turns to the Fella Bella and goes down on one knee, pulling a ring out of his pocket.

Policeman Mickey
Will you marry me? *(The crowd is open-mouthed, waiting for the Fella Bella's answer)*

The Fella Bella
Yes. *(The crowd all cheer and hug each other)*

Chief Superintendent
I can't believe this is happening. I've got two masked men holding a hostage at gun point, and I've got a police officer singing Shirley Bassey and proposing marriage. It's all madness.

Policeman Mickey
I must get back, but I'll see you tonight. I'm bringing passion fruit with me.

The Fella Bella
I can't wait *(the Fella Bella walks back to the hairdressers)*

Chief Superintendent
It's so nice of you to join us.

Policeman Mickey

You're welcome sir.

Phoebe

I've got an idea.

Mo

That sounds dangerous.

Phoebe

(Phoning Ben at the shop) Ben it's Mistress Phoebe here. I want you to collect up all the soap and Clearasil and bring it to the Post Office now, *(shouting)* Now!

Mo

No ships would hit rocks with your gob.

Two minutes later, Ben arrives with the soap and Clearasil.

Phoebe

Right *(to Ben)* give everyone a bar of soap and a bottle of Clearasil. Tell them when I shout throw, they all must throw the soap towards the Post Office. *(She kicks him up the bum and he goes on his way)*

Five minutes later a police officer walks towards the Post Office with the robbers' demands. He puts the food and Clearasil down about two metres away from the Post Office door, then walks away. Two minutes later, Filthy Phil comes out. He sticks two fingers up to the crowd and just as he picks the food up, Phoebe shouts "Throw!" With lots of soap bars flying through the air, several hit Filthy Phil on the head, and knocks him out. The crowd cheers. Seeing what has happened, Donkey Dick Dave (who is enraged) goes back into the Post Office and starts to threaten Zit Faced Zita. As her fears builds, the zits on her face starts to pop again. With this terrible sight, Donkey Dick Dave passes out on to the floor. Seeing this, Zit Faced Zita runs out of the Post Office into the street.

Zit Faced Zita
I'm free.

The crowd boos and throws bottles of Clearasil towards the Post Office. The police rush towards the robbers and handcuffs them. Two minutes later, they are seen taking the robbers away.

Mo
What an afternoon. It's been fun *(they all nod their heads)* Who would have thought a bar of soap would win the day?

Frigging Freda
And out of date soap at that.

Phoebe
I don't know what you mean. *(They all laugh)*

Frigging Freda
Right, I'm off to congratulate Bella.

Janice
Wait for me Freda, I'm booked in at four. *(They both walk off)*

Mo
While I remember, Chairman Harold wants us to attend our first board meeting a week next Tuesday.

Phoebe
Where are we meeting?

Mo
In the dungeon. It will be like home for you.

Phoebe

Cheeky cow. *(They all laugh)*

Mo

I'll see you then.

Phoebe

Bye Mo

Mo

Bye girls.

Mo is seen walking in the direction of the market.

The Board Meeting Today, The Grand Opening Tomorrow

Characters

Belter Bet
A medium sized woman in her mid-fifties. She is a lesbian, who has many tattoos that adorn her body.

Raging Ruth
A large woman in her late fifties. She gets angry at the smallest things. She is addicted to soap's.

Sharon
A small woman in her eighties. She has got a reputation of a woman you never cross, unless you want a smack in the mouth.

Darren
A tall nervous man in his late seventies. Despite the size of his wife, he is scared to death of her.

Other Characters
Mo, Phoebe, Carol, Harold, Vera Virus, Mini Meg, Pill Gill, and Penny pick a nose.

Setting
The Sarah Summers Museum

The Board Meeting Today, The Grand Opening Tomorrow

A table and chairs have been set up in the dungeon.

Harold

Right, come to order please. Thank you Mrs Bloomer. Now is not the time to hear about whether your husband looks better in boxers or Y-fronts. Besides, I'm more of a jock man myself. Well, good morning to you all, and welcome to our first board meeting. As you can see we have a lot to discuss, so let's get on with it. Item one, is the reports from each board member. Mrs Johnson, would you like to start.

Mo

Thank you Mr Chairman. Looking over the accounts in the last week, they do look very healthy. The bus company shows a surplus of around fifty thousand for the first year, with the slave membership being slightly up this year too, with a surplus of twenty thousand. Now taking into account gas, electric, water then we should have a surplus of around forty thousand. However, we do need to employ two and a half members of staff, so the profit margin will be around ten thousand.

Harold

So by the looks of it, we need to boost slave and visitor numbers.

Mo

Correct.

Harold

That moves us nicely on to our PR Mrs Winter-Bottom.

Vera Virus

Thank you Mr Chairman. Well, as you can see on my computer, we have just gone on-line with our very own app. You can see the lovely Mrs Bloomer in her wonderful outfit, showing us around each room of the museum.

Phoebe

Bloody hell, who chose that outfit?

Vera Virus

I did, I think it really shows of her assets.

Phoebe

Well, that's one way to describe it. Did they run out of fabric when it came to the top half?

Vera Virus

If you have got it, flaunt it.

Harold

Do continue Mrs Winter-Bottom. Thank you.

Vera Virus

Also, as you can see I have had a thousand posters made, with the lovely Mrs Bloomer modelling. You will find them in shops, pubs and even on buses. However, there have been a couple of accidents, due to some bus drivers getting distracted at the wheel.

Phoebe

I'm surprised it was just a couple.

Vera Virus

Although they are now starting to recruit a lot more women drivers, along with people from the LGBT community. This should make travelling safer. Despite this, the posters are a big hit with the passengers, with many people buying a day ticket to stay on the bus.

Harold
Thank you Mrs Winter-Bottom. I am impressed. Miss Dickson, would you like to tell us how recruitment is going?

Phoebe
Thank you Mr Chairman. Although I have been busy of late.

Mo
What, eating grapes?

Phoebe
How dare you.

Mo
Dick by name, dick by nature.

Phoebe
Shut it Johnson.

Mo
Piss off Dickson.

Harold
Right you two, off you go to the naughty step.

Both Mo and Phoebe go and sit on the dungeon steps, while Vera Virus and Carol can be seen laughing uncontrollably.

Carol
How old are those two.

Harold
Right, now you have calmed down, Miss Dickson can you give us your report. *(They both walk back to the table)*

Phoebe

Mr Chairman. As you know, Sarah did suggest Mini Meg to do the catering. So I went to see her last week and explained the situation. She said she was very happy to come on board and to leave all the ordering and recipes to her. She is expecting us all in the kitchen at one o'clock, so that we can sample some of her cuisine. She did say that her cookery class will be preparing a lot of the food, but she would need help in serving the food and using the till. She seemed very happy when I suggested Penny. Although I did say that she should keep her eyes on Penny's fingers at all times. As you know we have recruited the wonderful Mrs Bloomer as our tour guide, which I know she will be able to give them their money's worth. *(Everyone claps around the table)* Finally, we have had around a dozen applications for the job of dominatrix. They make Dracula look like Snow White. Our slaves need thrilling not killing. So I have whittled it down to three.

Mo

Who are those three Miss Dickson?

Phoebe

Belter Bet, and Raging Ruth. They are two women in their fifties.

Mo

The third one?

Phoebe

Pill Gill.

Carol

Who?

Phoebe

Pill Gill?

Harold

Who, our Pill Gill?

Phoebe

That's right. She goes under the name of 'Wonder Revenge.'

Mo

What's all that about?

Phoebe

Well, you know how she was seeing that bloke who thought he was Spider Man?

Mo

Yes.

Phoebe

Well, apparently, he cast his web much wider and he's the father of a lot of baby spiders - finding out about this, when Spider-Man was flying towards Wonder Woman's window she shut the window on him. The broken glass just missed his heart, but sliced off his manhood. As he was rolling around the bedroom in agony, Pill Gill said, "If only you had the heart to tell me, you could have still been Spider Man But without your manhood, you can't put the man into Spider Man. The world wide web crashed and gone from you."

Vera Virus

I can see why she has applied for the job.

Vera Virus

Thank you Miss Dickson. It's amazing how much you can achieve with so much time on your hands. As you know, we have priced the visitors admission, at ten pounds but we really do need to push the membership.

Carol

I'll push them all the way.

Harold

You can push any man that was six foot away with your assets *(they all laugh)* Right, I think it's time for lunch. Are there any more points to be discussed? *(They all have their mouths open to speak)* Meeting adjourned. I'm starving.

They all head towards the kitchen, where there is a ribbon across the entrance to the kitchen.

Mini Meg

Mrs Johnson, would you like to say a few words and cut the ribbon?

Mo

Thank you Meg, I would be delighted.

Phoebe

Here she goes.

Mo

I want to thank you all for coming and knowing what a great team we are, I know we will go on to greatness, serving the people of this community.

Phoebe

Your Oscar is in the post.

Mo

I now pronounce the 'Four Seasons' cafe open. *(Everyone claps)*

Mini Meg

I have set up a table in the middle.

Harold

Thank you Meg. *(They all sit down)*

Vera Virus

Why have we called it the 'Four Seasons' cafe?

Harold

With Sarah's surname being Summers, we thought it was a nice touch. Although the darkness and coldness of winter would have suited more.

Mini Meg and Penny come to the table with menus.

Mini Meg

Hello everyone *(passing the menus out)* As you can see, we have a variety of choices.

Harold

It looks very impressive Meg, I'll have the chicken hotpot.

Vera Virus

Me too.

Carol

And me.

Mini Meg

That's three hot pots. Miss Dickson?

Phoebe

I'll have the meat and potato pie.

Mo

I would have thought you get enough meat.

Phoebe
You can never have too much meat in your day.

Mini Meg
Mrs Johnson?

Mo
I'll have the omelette.

Mini Meg
What filling would you like?

Mo
I don't usually have a filling *(everyone bursts out laughing)* cheese would be good.

Ten minutes later, the food is brought over.

Harold
That looks wonderful Meg.

Mini Meg
Thank you Mr Castle.

Harold
I hope you are keeping in budget?

Mini Meg
I am Mr Castle.

Harold
How do you make such good food, at such low prices?

Mini Meg
Well, a lot of it is made at my cookery class, so it keeps the prices down. For examples, the chicken and eggs are very cheap to buy.

Harold

Why is that?

Mini Meg

Well, one of my ladies is a farmer's wife, who twice a week likes to role play with her husband.

Harold

How does that work?

Mini Meg

Well, she dresses up as 'Little Red Riding Hood' and with her red cape on and her basket on her arm, she walks to Grandma's cottage. As she walks past the chicken coup, her husband, dressed up as a wolf, stops her and says, "Hello, who are you, and where are you going?" His wife says, "I'm Little Red Riding Hood, and I'm taking my virgin self off to see Grandma." The wolf says, "What have you got in your basket, Little Red Riding Hood?" She tells him "A pack of ribbed johnnies, some lube and an eight inch dildo." The wolf says, "You don't get that in a basket every day." To which Red Riding Hood replies "Well, Grandma has got a new boyfriend who is bisexual, so she likes to cover every avenue." Anyway, the wolf runs off and 'Little Red Riding Hood' walks around the field and back to the farm house. She then changes into Grandma and gets into bed. Ten minutes later, the 'wolf' knocks on her bedroom door. Grandma says, "Is that you, Little Red Riding Hood? With my essentials?" Her husband replies "It is Grandma (her husband walks into the room as Little Red Riding Hood). Grandma says, "What big eyes you have." Little Red Riding Hood replies, "All the better to see every inch of your naked body." Then Grandma says "What big hands you have," Little Red Riding Hood says "All the better to hold your large breasts." Then Grandma says ,"What a lot of hair you have." Little Red Riding Hood replies "To show you what a real man I am." He rips off his outfit and dives on to Grandma. Ten minutes later, the woodcutter runs into the bedroom with his big chopper. He is played by the farmer in the next farm. The

Woodcutter says, "What are you doing Grandma?" Grandma replies, "He is giving me a good seeing to. Get down here and pick a hole." The Woodcutter picks the husbands hole - now you can see that in Little Red Riding Hood's basket, every avenue was covered.

Harold
But, what has that got to do with the price of eggs and chickens?

Mini Meg
Well, the wolf always stops 'Little Red Riding Hood' outside of the chicken coup. Seeing the wolf outside, freaks the hens out. They either get rid of all their eggs or they die of shock. Hence the reason why the price is so low.

Harold
That was amazing Meg. Right everyone. It's back to the dungeon for our first audition.

They all get up from the table and, thanking Meg, walk down to the dungeon

Harold
(Sitting down) Right, we have got our slaves in place, lets have the first one.

Phoebe brings in the first candidate, guiding her to her seat.

Harold
Good afternoon Miss Painly.

Belter Bet
Call me Belter, all men do.

Harold
Now Miss Belter, why do you want this position?

Belter Bet

To be honest with you, I could do with the extra money.

Harold

Not as it's any of my business, but why is that?

Belter Bet

I need to get a new tattoo put on my whipping hand.

Harold

Really, what sort of tattoo?

Belter Bet

It's a poem.

Harold

That sounds nice. What will it say?

Belter Bet

'Hating all men is good, men are bad, whipping their ass, will make me glad.'

Harold

That's very interesting Miss Belter. Anyone else got any questions?

Mo

There maybe times when we might need you to do some overtime. Would that be alright?

Belter Bet

Not really love - you see I'm a dressmaker who likes to design and make dresses for women to wear when they visit me for sex.

Harold

Right, shall we get started? As you can see the slaves are all ready, so it's over to you.

Belter Bet walks over to the middle of the dungeon and begins.

Phoebe
The way she goes on, anyone would think she is doing us a favour.

Vera Virus
Well, she's been at it for ten minutes now and there are two slaves, still standing around with nothing to do and with all this dust in here.

Carol
She's going for the rack *(a phone starts to ring)* whose phone is that? *(Everyone looks to see if it's their phone. Belter Bet starts talking on her phone, whilst the slave on the rack is yawning)*

Mo
It seems that we are getting in the way of her social life.

Harold rings the bell and Belter Bet returns back to the table.

Belter Bet
Sorry about the phone call. It was me mate wanting to know if we are going out on a bender tonight.

Harold
Thank you for coming Miss Belter, we will let you know. *(She walks out the room)*

Phoebe
(Ripping up her application) Well that was a waste of time.

Vera Virus
But she won't be able to get her tattoo now.

Phoebe
She will have to get a smaller one with just four letters.

Mo
What will that be?

Phoebe
Twat. *(They all laugh)*

Harold
Right, Miss Dickson can we have the next one please.

Phoebe goes and fetches the next applicant.

Harold
Good afternoon Miss Angerly.

Raging Ruth
Just call me Raging.

Harold
So why do you want the job?

Raging Ruth
If you don't mind can we skip the questions, I've had a very bad morning.

Harold
What has happened?

Raging Ruth
Firstly, they have stopped the morning re-runs of 'EastEnders' and changed it to 'Mastermind.' I can't answer one of those frigging questions. Secondly I forgot to put my underwear on a boil wash.

Mo

There may be some times when we might need you to work some overtime, would that be alright?

Raging Ruth

If it's going to stop me from watching the soaps, then no. I had an audition once, for one of them soaps.

Mo

How did it go?

Raging Ruth

Not very well. Another thing that had made me very angry is they have stopped the re-runs of 'Emmerdale' and replaced it with 'A Question of Sport.' Do I look like a person who plays sports?

Harold

There's always shot put.

Raging Ruth

Are you taking the piss?

Phoebe

Shall we make a start?

Raging Ruth

Shall we not. *(She gets up and walks out)*

Vera Virus

Well that one was a raging nutter.

Carol

She could do with a re-run of her life, so she could sort it out.

Mo

Samaritans comes to mind.

Harold

Well, Pill Gill to go. Much more of this and I'll be taking an overdose. Phoebe, would you please go and fetch Miss Wonders. *(Phoebe goes to collect her and brings her in)*

Pill Gill

Hello everybody, it's been a long time.

Mo

Too long, I've heard you have been having a few problems?

Pill Gill

Men, Mrs Johnson. How could any man cheat on 'Wonder Woman.' I gave him everything. My juices were flowing when he stuck his spiders fangs into me. I even grew my breasts, for when the little spider babies came along. Well, he won't be mating anyone now, now this black widow has done her thing. But what really upset me Mrs Johnson, is the fact that he nearly lost me my identity as 'Wonder Woman.'

Mo

So why do you want this job?

Pill Gill

To show that Mistress Wonders is back and that no man will mess with my identity again.

Phoebe

Shall we make a start? *(Pill Gill walks to the middle of the dungeon and in a loud voice, she begins)*

Harold

I can see she is still as mad as a hatter, but all the slaves are on task.

Pill Gill

(To one of the slaves in a deep voice) I'll show you what we do to lazy slaves *(she gets hold of the slave by his hair and drags him to the whipping wall. She is seen whipping his naked bottom)*

Phoebe

She is showing good observational skills.

Pill Gill

Slave, put your back into it.

Slave

I am Mistress Wonders.

Pill Gill

Don't you talk back to me you vile creature *(she gets hold of his nose and drags him to the rock. As she moves the wheel, the slave can be heard screaming)*

Carol

Well, she is entertaining me.

Harold

(He rings the bell) Come back and join us Miss Wonders.

Pill Gill comes over and sits down.

Mo

Well, Miss Wonders, you have shown excellent observational skills and you didn't let any of the slaves get the better of you. Now, I do need to ask you, there may be times when we might need you to do some overtime, would that be alright?

Pill Gill

That would be fine. In fact, I was wondering if it was possible that you could supply accommodation with the job?

Harold

There is a spare room on the ground floor.

Vera Virus

It would be good to have someone on the premises at all times.

Phoebe

Why do you need accommodation?

Pill Gill

As you know I've been staying with my sister and it's not the fact that Spider Man flew into my bedroom window or that his manhood was sliced off, but the fact that she is having problems matching up the new glass to match all the other windows in the bungalow. So she wants me out.

Mo

With a reduced rate for your board and lodgings, I think we can sort something out.

Pill Gill

Does that mean I have got the job?

Harold

If you can start tomorrow, you have got the job.

Pill Gill hugs everyone and as she walks through the door, the slaves are seen clapping.

Phoebe

It's like 'Goldilocks and the Three Bears.' It was Baby Bear that was just right.

Carol

Answer me one thing.

Mo
What's that?

Carol
If she lives in a bungalow, why does she say that Spider Man flies though the window and not climb through the window?

Mo
Because Spider Man, with the help of his web, flies.

Carol
But...

Mo
Carol love, in Gill's fantasy role playing mind, that's what he does. Talking of Baby Bear whose porridge is just right, my two will be waiting for their teas. I'll see you all tomorrow for the grand opening. *(Mo hugs and kisses everyone as she leaves)*

The Grand Opening

Harold
Well, ladies, the day has arrived. I've heard there is a queue around the block. Carol, get yourself out here so we can see your outfit.

Carol walks out, showing she is wearing black suspenders and knee high boots. She also has on a tight low cut dress that barely covers her breasts.

Mo
Carol you look amazing.

Phoebe

You were born to do this job.
Vera Virus
You are sex appeal.

Harold
Make sure they don't pop out. Our licence doesn't cover that sort of entertainment. Right everyone, to your posts. *(They all move to their position and Harold opens the door)*

Everyone pays Vera Virus their entrance fee and stands in the entrance hall waiting for the tour guide. Carol appears and the visitors eyes fall onto Carol's outfit.

Carol
Good afternoon everyone and welcome to the Sarah Summers Museum. I will tell you a little bit about the history of the house and then I will take you on a tour, showing you each of the rooms. Now, the house was built in the mid 19th century and is built over three floors. The servants quarters are at the top of the house, with the bedrooms of the family on the first floor. The house had various occupants over the years with Sarah and her husband moving in to the house in 1963. Employing a couple of domestics, who lived in, they were both very happy for the first two years. But Sarah developed a dryness down below and penetration became painful. So her young husband found a dark passage at the back of that house that led to the domestic's bedrooms. Before long, he was going down the dark passages at least once a day. Six months later, he and the domestics left, leaving Sarah penniless and all alone. Sarah knew she had to act quickly to save herself. Walking down the dark passage, an idea sprung into her mind. When the young gardener came the next morning, she asked him to get rid of the weeds. Being a young man, with girls on his mind, he didn't rush, until Sarah kicked up the bum and shouted at him to work faster. The weeding was done in no time at all, so she made a point of kicking him up the bottom. The garden won awards. So the dark passage and the gardener's bottom being kicked, allowed Sarah to

build her empire that you see today. Right everyone, follow me and we will descend the stairs, to the top floor. *(They all follow Carol to the top floor)* As you can see, although the bedrooms are small, there is good light and ventilation and before you ask, Sarah's husband was a small man. We are going to go down the dark passage to Sarah's bedroom. *(As they start to walk one of the visitors can be heard talking to her husband)*

Sharon

Look at her tits again and you will go down the dark passage, arse over tit. To think I went on the pill last year because rubber was giving you erection problems.

Darren

You know I only have eyes for you.

Sharon

Keep it that way or you won't have any eyes to see with.

Mo

(Whispering at the back of the line to Phoebe) And she means it. Back in the day, I've seen her take out body builders. She was known as the female Rocky.

Phoebe

How old is she?

Mo

She was eighty last Christmas.

Carol

(Standing half way along the dark passage) Please don't forget you can be a part of this wonderful history as a member. *(They arrive at Sarah's bedroom)* As you can see, Sarah's bedroom is richly decorated. She loved the finer things in life. But she never forgot what made her, hence the reason for her dominatrix outfits that

she had framed, that are hanging on her walls. Right everyone, I have had a message from Mistress Wonders that she is ready for us in the dungeon. *(Carol takes them down the dungeon and sits them down)* Ladies and gentleman, enjoy the wonderful Mistress Wonders. *(As Gill gets going, Carol leaves the dungeon and appears in the hallway to be greeted by the other committee members)*

Mo
Carol you were amazing.

Phoebe
You were incredible girl. *(They all give her a hug)*

Vera Virus
Do you know I've got ten signed up already and it's only the first day.

Harold
Well ladies, I think that's what we can call a successful day and Carol, where did you get that story from?

Carol
My Tony didn't put the papers in the right bin, so I kicked him up the bum. He gets it right every time now. *(They all laugh)* Right, I think they have had their half hour, it's time to flog the food.

Carol gets back into the dungeon and rings the bell to signal the end of the performance. On the way to the kitchen, Mo can hear the praise from the visitors as they walk to the kitchen. Seeing that the job was done for now, Mo walks out of the door and down the street with a smile on her face.

Sink or Swim

Characters

Miss Lovelace
A tall good looking woman in her early thirties. She is the mother of Caroline. As a single mother, she is man mad.

Mrs Smith
A small woman in her mid thirties. She is the mother of Robert. She is financially well off and likes to brag about it, but she doesn't have a good sense of humour.

Bus driver
A plump man in his forties. He fancies himself as a ladies man.

Other Characters
Mo, Mr M, Mr Browny, Mr Woody, Miss Roach, Miss Archer, Charlie, Billy Miss Bigwood and all the children.

Setting
The classroom, the coach and the swimming baths.

Sink or Swim

Mr M walks into the classroom.

Mr M

Good morning you gorgeous lady. How are you?

Mo

Hello Mr M *(they hug)* I'm very well, I hope you are?

Mr M

I'm as well as I can be, being a teacher.

Mo

How's your writing going?

Mr M

It's going well. My second book has just come out and I'm writing my third one, although this will be the last one. I think three books about a village and its occupants is enough for any reader.

Mo

Make sure you get me a copy. If it's as good as the first one then I'm in for a treat.

Mr M

You are a star. Although the new book is a pound extra, I'm only going to charge you the same as I did for the first one, a fiver. I've got to look after my loyal fans.

Mo

I'm definitely one of those.

Mr M

Mind you, what with funerals, museums and robberies, your

life is never boring and its not even Easter yet! *(They both laugh)*

Mo
It's just a normal year in the life of a village girl.

Mr M
I went to the Post Office the other day. I must admit, Zit Faced Zita's zits didn't look that bad. She must be using all that Clearasil the crowd threw at her.

Mo
Zita always did like a freebie. Before you could match up all the spots and it would make a picture of a swan. But with the spots fading, she's back to being the ugly duckling again. *(They both laugh)*

Mr M
Tell it how it is girl.

Miss Roach comes through the door.

Mo
Good morning Miss Roach.

Miss Roach
Morning Mrs Johnson.

Mr M
You been on the piss again?

Miss Roach
I only had a couple.

Mr M
What, a couple of pints of Vodka?

Miss Roach

Mr M, anyone would think I was an alcoholic.

Mr M

How many times have you been out this week?

Miss Roach

Every night.

Mr M

How many times did you go out last week?

Miss Roach

Every night.

Mr M

And as you are still walking bow-legged, you must be still seeing Donkey Dan?

Miss Roach

He reaches parts that nobody can.

Mr M

With a ten inch penis, he will do.

Miss Roach

But he does make me feel really special. I shouldn't say, but the other day we had a threesome with another woman.

Mr M

How did he make you feel special with another woman there?

Miss Roach

He took her from behind, but he took me from the front. As he says, he loves to look into my eyes as I'm screaming. How special is that.

Mr M

Let's make this morning special, with the children seeing you awake for all of it. Look busy, Miss Bigwood is on her way.

Miss Bigwood

Good morning everyone *(she goes over to hug Mo)* it's great to see you again Mrs Johnson.

Mo

It's always great to be back.

Miss Bigwood

Mr M, can you come and see me at dinner time? I need to know if you an do next week for Mr Woody's class.

Mr M

Is he not well?

Miss Bigwood

If being ecstatic that you are going on a course to find out what are the best woods for building with, then I would say he's not well at all.

Mr M

The Titanic comes to mind.

Miss Bigwood

Walking the plank comes to my mind. *(As she is walking to the door, she spots Miss Roach)* Miss Roach, are you going in the water with the children this morning?

Miss Roach

Yes Miss Bigwood.

Miss Bigwood

Make sure you put arm bands on each arm. With all the alcohol you consume, we don't want you sinking like your career. *(Miss Bigwood walks out of the classroom)*

Miss Roach

Cow. Just because I like a glass of wine now and again.

Mr M

Don't you mean bottles again and again Miss Roach? Anyway, I've been left no planning, so after register, we will do some spelling, which will take us up to assembly. Who's doing assembly Miss Roach?

Miss Roach

I think it's Mr Woody.

Mr M

Well that assembly has sunk before it starts. Then it's off to swimming at ten thirty. Have we got a couple of parents coming to blow the horns?

Miss Roach

Robert's mum, Mrs Smith.

Mr M

Bloody hell, she will be blowing her own horn then, that one.

Miss Roach

Miss Lovelace.

Mr M

The only blow she can do is a blow job. Make sure you sit next to me, Miss Roach, on the bus. Lovelace's hands will be all over me like a rash. Right, it is time to go and let the little darlings in. Go on Mrs Johnson, you can do the honours.

Mo

(Walking over to the door, she opens it.) Hello everyone *(all the children shout hello and hug Mo as they walk by her)*

Mr M

Good morning everyone. Go and put your coats and swimming bags on your pegs. *(The children do this, then come and sit on the carpet.)* Well, here we all are. Let Mr M get his register. I need a red pen and a black pen *(looking in his brief case)* found them. Lucy good morning.

Lucy

Good morning Mr M. You smell nice Mr M.

Mr M

Thank you Lucy love. It's Prada. Not cheap, but you have to treat yourself sometimes. For some it's bottles of wine *(looking at Miss Roach)* for others it's beautiful clothes. *(He looks at Mo. Mo winks)* For me, it's a nice aftershave. Come and have a smell. *(Lucy smells Mr M's aftershave)*

Lucy

Beautiful Mr M.

Mr M

A team point for Lucy, for showing excellent taste. Everyone let's sing Lucy's song. *(All the children do this)* James good morning.

James

Good morning Mr M. Wonderful shoes Mr M.

Mr M

Thank you James. As you can see, they are new. I brought them because they look good with both trousers and jeans.

James

Good choice Mr M.

Mr M

A team point for James, for showing he knows about style. Good morning Gary.

Gary

Good morning Mr M.

Mr M

How's your mum?

Gary

She is so excited Mr M.

Mr M

Is she, why's that then?

Gary

She is having a tattoo of a large snake on her leg.

Mr M

That sounds wonderful. Have you had any breakfast this morning?

Gary

No Mr M.

Mr M

Come and see me at break time. Caroline good morning.

Caroline

Good morning Mr M.

Mr M

How's that mother of yours?

Caroline

She is getting very excited.

Mr M

Is she. What brought that on?

Caroline

She is going out in a few weeks with her mates and she went to see a fortune teller. She told her she is going to meet the man of her dreams.

Mr M

Did the fortune teller forget to clean her crystal ball, or was she expecting a tip? Good morning Valerie.

Valerie

Good morning Mr M. Mr M your waist coat looks a bit tight.

Mr M

It's not as tight as your time will be in the water. Good morning Jeremy.

Jeremy

Good morning Mr M.

Mr M

I bet you didn't recognise Miss Roach with her eyes open. I'm sure Miss Roach will miss the one to one time you gave her. Good morning Aegeus.

Aegeus

Good morning Mr M.

Mr M

Who's your father this week?

Aegeus

We all went to visit a farm last week, where there was a lot of sheep. Daddy thinks he is 'Little Bo Peep' now.

Mr M

Knowing your family, he must be the black sheep of the family by now *(Aegeus nods his head)* Good morning Robert.

Robert

Good morning Mr M.

Mr M

Is your mother still seeing spirits?

Robert

Yes Mr M. She kept looking at a bottle of gin in the cupboard. Two hours later she tripped over the dog and knocked out two of her teeth, She has not been able to speak for the last two days.

Mr M

Well that's a blessing for us all. Good morning Johnny.

Johnny

Good morning Mr M. I've got a message from my mum.

Mr M

What's that?

Johnny

She said do you need any knock off aftershave?

Mr M

What's she got?

Johnny

Gautier 2, Prada and Allure Chanel. For the women, she has got Lady Million and Prada Woman.

Mr M

How much?

Johnny

A tenner each.

Mr M

I'll have all three of the men's. Miss Roach?

Miss Roach

I'll have one each of the woman's. All this going out, I've not got much left.

Mr M

Mrs Johnson?

Mo

I'll have one each of the woman's.

Mr M

I'll write your mum a list Johnny and put it in your bag. Tell your mum to come and see me, I'll be in Mr Woody's class next week. I'll pop yours round Mrs Johnson.

Mo

You are kind Mr M.

Mr M

Good morning Mabel.

Mabel

Good morning Mr M.

Mr M

Mabel, when you have got time, can you put a damp cloth over my car? I forgot to put the bird seed out and they are getting their revenge.

Mabel

Leave it with me Mr M.

Mr M

Zeeta and Rita, good morning.

Zeeta/Rita

Good morning Mr M.

Mr M

You both well girls?

Zeeta/Rita

Yes thank you Mr M.

Mr M

Are you both happy?

Zeeta/Rita

We are both happy Mr M.

Mr M

Now that is togetherness Mrs Johnson.

Valerie

You speak for yourself.

Mr M

Thank you Valerie. Good morning Amy.

Amy

Good morning Mr M.

Mr M

How's the baby?

Amy

She is very beautiful Mr M. Mind you, it should be. The length of time it took mummy to push her out.

Mr M

It was a good job you were there Amy.

Amy

It was Mr M. If it wasn't for me shouting 'bleeding push' the baby would still be in there.

Mr M

Wonderful. Good morning my two super boys.

David

Good morning Mr M.

Marvin

Good morning Mr M.

Mr M

What's been happening with you two?

Marvin

Grandma is coming from Jamaica to visit for two weeks, but she has got such a strong accent I don't think I will understand her.

Mr M

Remember, Grandmas are the best cooks, so you will understand her, through her amazing food she cooks.

James

How is Kevin the cat?

Valerie

We don't care.

Mr M

But we all do care Valerie, just like we care about you sitting there being rude. So you know where the door is, go and walk through it, to the dark side - off you go. *(Valerie stands up and walks through the door)* That reminds me, Lucy can you go to Mr Browny's class and ask him to send Charlie with the book. *(Lucy goes off)* Now everyone it's spelling time. So go and find your places and Miss Roach will hand out your spelling books. *(The children go to their places and Miss Roach gives them their books. Charlie, the year 6, comes into the classroom.)*

Charlie

Good morning Mr M.

Mr M

Good morning Charlie. I can see you've brought me the book. How much?

Charlie

One pound twenty.

Mr M

Where has the extra twenty pence come from?

Charlie

It's the budget Mr M. She has to pass on the extra to the customer. As my mum says, 'she hasn't got bleeding Oxfam painted on her forehead.'

Mr M

Here's your extra twenty pence *(Charlie walks out the door)* Right, where was I, spellings. Miss Roach, you better let Valerie back in. *(Valerie comes in and sits down at her table)* Now, because we have been looking at describing words, I thought we could use one word to describe a member of staff and then write a sentence with the word in it. Mr M.

Robert

Wonderful.

Mr M

The sentence?

Robert

Mr M is a wonderful teacher.

Mr M

A team point for Robert. So everyone, spell wonderful. Next person, Miss Roach.

Valerie

Pissed.

Mr M

I can see where you are coming from, but I need another word.

Jeremy

Needy.

Mr M

The sentence?

Jeremy

Miss Roach is always needy after a skin full the night before.

Mr M

I love it Jeremy, everybody spell needy. The next person is Mrs Johnson.

Lucy

Loaded.

Mr M

You're on the right lines, but I need another word.

Marvin

Nice.

Mr M

The sentence?

Marvin

Mrs Johnson is nice when she is loaded. *(Mo laughs)*

Mr M

That sounds great. Everyone spell nice. The next one is Mr Woody.

Amy

Boring.

Mr M

The sentence?

Amy

Mr Woody is so boring I would rather watch paint dry.

Mr M

That is very honest Amy. Everyone spell boring. The next one is Mr Browny.

Johnny

Hands.

Mr M

The sentence?

Johnny

Mr Browny is very hands-on around female members of staff.

Mr M

Very observant Johnny. Everyone spell hands. Right, a couple more. Miss Archer.

Aegeus

Heavy.

Mr M

The sentence?

Aegeus

Miss Archer is very top heavy.

Mr M

I've never noticed that.

Valerie

You need to have your eyes tested.

Mr M

Thank you Valerie. Everyone spell heavy. The last one, Miss Bigwood.

Rita

Frightening.

Mr M

The sentence?

Rita

Miss Bigwood is frightening when she is telling her staff off.

Mr M

I'm sure Miss Roach can relate to that. Everyone spell frightening.

Miss Archer

(Comes into the class) It's assembly time Mr M.

Mr M

Thank you Miss Archer. As you go to line up, pass your spelling books to Mrs Johnson who I'm sure will enjoy marking them. I'm sure Miss Roach will enjoy helping you Mrs Johnson, or would you like to go to Mr Woody's assembly?

Miss Roach

I'll look after Mrs Johnson.

Mr M

I thought you would. Right everyone, line up *(the children do this)* Lets go. *(They walk to the hall and sit down. Mr M sits next to Mr Browny)*

Mr Browny

How's it going Mr M?

Mr M

It was going fine until I heard it was Mr Woody's assembly.

Mr Browny

I know what you mean, it's like watching paint dry.

Mr M

That's how one of my children described him.

Mr Woody

Good morning children.

Everyone

Good morning Mr Woody, good morning everyone.

Mr Woody

Now, I know you all are enjoying my assemblies on boats and boat building.

Mr Browny

(*Whispering*) Is he taking the piss?

Mr Woody

So I thought we would look at how Vikings made their boats.

Mr M

(*Whispering*) Bloody hell. That reminds me, what's this extra twenty pence extra for a fag all about?

Mr Browny

He gave me some spiel. The only thing stamped on her forehead is slut.

Mr M

I've got swimming next, so I'm off for my break. See you later.

Mr M goes off for his cigarette and ten minutes later, he comes back to collect the children.

Mr Browny

You didn't miss anything other than half the children falling asleep.

Mr M

Who needs sleeping tablets when you have got Woody *(they both laugh)* Right children, stand. *(The children stand up and walk back to the classroom)* Get your coats and swimming bags and line up at the door *(the children do this)* Miss Roach and Mrs Johnson, are you ready?

Miss Roach

We are.

Mr M

That's good to hear. But before we go we have a special helper, he's coming through the door now. Good morning Billy.

Billy

Good morning Mr M.

Mr M

Would you like to walk next to Mrs Johnson? She looks as though she could be trouble. *(Smiling, Billy gives Mo a hug)* Miss Roach, where are the parent helpers?

Miss Roach

They are here Mr M. *(They both get on to the bus)*

Mr M

Come on girls, it will be Christmas before we get going. Usain Bolt has got nothing to worry about. *(Miss Lovelace sits next to Mr M)* Right driver, when you are ready. *(The bus drives off)*

Miss Lovelace

I didn't think I would get to sit next to a big strong man like you Mr M. *(She puts her hand on Mr M's leg)*

Mr M

I didn't either Miss Lovelace.

Miss Lovelace

Lucy is at her dad's this weekend, so why don't you pop round for a bite to eat. You will love dessert.

Mr M

I would love to Miss Lovelace, but I'm washing my hair tonight.

Miss Lovelace

I could help you wash your chest hair and I bet you have a nice bush down below, that needs a good wash.

Mr M

That's very kind of you to offer. Bus driver, have you got any music? *(The bus driver switches his radio on and 'Love Is In The Air' is playing).* Can it get any worse.

Miss Lovelace

They are playing our song big boy.

Mr M

(Caroline begins to cry a couple of seats back) Excuse me Miss Lovelace, I must go and see what the problem is *(Mr M walks down the bus to Caroline)* What's a matter flower?

Caroline

I want mummy to sit next to me.

Mr M

(Shouting) Miss Lovelace, your daughter wants you. Robert *(who is sitting next to Caroline)* get yourself up the front.

Robert

Do I have to?

Mr M

If you want to see a playtime next week then yes. *(Miss Lovelace and Robert swap places. Mr M goes and sits down)*

Robert
That Lovelace woman is a bit hands on.

Mr M
She's like a rash that gets everywhere.

Bus Driver
She could put cream on my rash any day. You couldn't give her my number mate?

Mr M
Do I look like a dating agency?

Bus Driver
Go on mate.

Mr M
Go on then, give me a couple of fags for doing it.

Bus Driver
You're a star mate.

Mr M
A fallen one. *(The bus driver arrives at the swimming baths)* Right everyone, if you are a wonderful girl, follow Miss Roach. *(The girls follow Miss Roach)* The boys follow me. Thank you bus driver. *(The bus driver hands Mr M his phone number and a couple of fags)* Mrs Johnson can you check no-one left anything behind?

Mo
Will do Mr M.

The boys stand next to the girls at the front of the swimming baths.

Mr M

Have you counted up Miss Roach?

Miss Roach

They are all here Mr M.

Mr M

Right, off you go. The wonderful parent helpers, would you like to follow. *(They both walk in with the girls)* Right Miss Johnson, if you would like to bring up the rear, off we go. *(They walk to the boys changing rooms)* Here's our room. Billy, do you want your own cubicle?

Billy

Yes please Mr M.

Mr M

Off you pop then. When you are ready, go and sit down next to the pool. *(All the children do this)* Now we are all here, we are going to swim two widths of the baths. There and back, there and back. Wait a minute, let's wait for Miss Roach to get in. *(Miss Roach climbs down the steps and loses her footing. She falls into the water and sinks to the bottom. Her bikini top comes off and floats to the top of the water. Two of the male attendants jump in to save her)* What that woman does to get some male attention. *(The attendants fix Miss Roach's bikini top under the water and Miss Roach comes to the surface)* Now that Miss Roach has sorted her weekend out, off you go. *(The children walk down the step and swim over to the other side)* I say Billy, those swimming trunks look a bit pink.

Billy

Aunty Mo put them in the water with her red smalls.

Mr M

(Looking at Mo) Did she now. *(Mo goes bright red. Mr M sees*

Gary walking down the steps) Gary come and have a chat with Mr M. *(They sit together)* Now Gary you super boy, what's been happening with your back and legs? *(With tears in his eyes, he doesn't say a word)* Did your step dad come round last night?

Gary
He was drunk and kept hitting mummy. I accidentally knocked over one of his beer bottles. He took off his belt and just kept hitting me with it. I could feel the blood running down my back. It's so painful Mr M. *(Gary hugs Mr M)*

Mr M
We are going to make sure this never happens again my darling. *(A tear runs down Mr M's cheek)* Miss Roach I need to make a phone call. Can you keep an eye on them?

Miss Roach
Will do.

Mr M
Mrs Johnson, will you get Gary's towel please and then sit with him.

Mo
Yes of course I will.

Mr M goes to the end of the swimming baths and phones the school. Putting his phone on loud speaker, he speaks to the secretary.

Mr M
Hello, it's Mr M, is Miss Bigwood there?

Mrs Evans
She is, but she's in a meeting.

Mr M

Could you get her out of the meeting and to the phone please.

Mrs Evans

I think they have nearly finished.

Mr M

(In a loud voice) I couldn't care less if she is nearly finished or just starting, get her to the phone now!

Mrs Evans

There is no need to shout.

Mr M

Now Mrs Evans.

There is a minute's silence and then Mrs Bigwood comes to the phone.

Miss Bigwood

What's happening Mr M?

Mr M

Gary Pritched has taken a severe beating from his stepfather. He has got open wounds that are bleeding. He also has severe bruising on his legs. He needs to go to hospital and the police need to be notified.

Miss Bigwood

I'm on my way Mr M. Ten minutes. *(Mr M joins the children)*

Mr M

Right everyone, come and sit on the edge of the pool *(the children do this)* Now what we are going to do today is some life saving skills. Billy, I want you to flap your arms around and shout for help. Then Miss Roach will rush to save you. It will be like 'Bay

Watch.' Off you go. Can you see children, Miss Roach has gone under Billy's body and has her hand underneath his chin, so the water doesn't go into his mouth. Wonderful you two. Right, find a partner and each of you take it in turns. *(They all take it in turns)* Ladies they are doing wonderfully.

Miss Bigwood races in and heads straight over to Gary. Mr M walks over.

Mo
He keeps falling asleep. I think the pain has kept him up most of the night.

Mr M
Gary stand up for me. *(As he stands up Miss Bigwood gasps)*

Miss Bigwood
This is shocking Mr M.

Mr M
In twenty-six years of teaching I've never seen anything like it.

Miss Bigwood
Let's get some clothes on you young man and then you can have a ride in Miss Bigwood's car.

Mr M
Now that is a special treat.

Miss Bigwood
I need you to write a report as soon as you get back. Then you need to take Mr Woody's class this afternoon.

Mr M
I'll be there. *(Miss Bigwood hugs Mr M)*

Miss Bigwood
I'll see you all later *(she walks out with Gary)*

Mr M
(Walking back to the children) Right everyone, as you are all wonderful you can all have five minutes of play. *(In the middle of the pool, Jeremy is having problems keeping afloat. Billy is playing with the black brick)* Billy, put the brick down and save Jeremy. *(Billy doesn't hear. In a loud voice)* Billy drop the brick and get a hold of Jeremy. *(Billy drops the brick and life saves Jeremy, the way he was taught. Mr M helps Jeremy up the steps)* Are you out of breath flower? Come and have a sit down and get your breath back. *(He sits down)* Right everyone, it's time to go and because you have all been so wonderful, five team points for everyone *(the children cheer Billy is the last one to get out of the pool)* and for you young man, fifty team points and a special journey to the shops, so that Aunty Mo can buy you a special present.

Billy
Thanks Mr M.

Mr M
Now go and give Aunty Mo a hug and then off you go to get dressed. *(Billy does this)* Thank you ladies you were wonderful.

Mo
Thank you Mr M.

The coach pulls up outside the school.

Mr M
Our two wonderful parent helpers would you like to descend first *(This they do with Mr M)* Miss Lovelace, this is for you *(he gives her a piece of paper with the bus drivers number on it)*

Miss Lovelace
I'll call you later Mr M.

Mr M
Right come on then everyone. Mrs Johnson can you check no-one has left anything?

Mo
Will do.

Mr M
Miss Roach can you count the children as they get off please.

Miss Roach
Will do.

The children follow Mr M into the classroom.

Mr M
Coats and bags on your pegs then line up for dinner. *(The children do this. The dinner lady comes in)* Good morning Mrs Cartwright. There's one short, Gary Pritched.

Mrs Cartwright
Thank you Mr M. *(The children walk off for dinner)*

Mr M
Well, what a morning.

Mo
How do you do it Mr M?

Mr M
Experience I think Mrs Johnson. I better go and write this report. Thank you again Mrs Johnson. I'm sure you will be coming to a special assembly next week. You have got a fine boy there.

Mo

I'm very lucky to have him.

Mr M

He is very lucky to have you. See you soon. *(They hug, and Mr M walks out of the class)*

Mo

(Getting her coat and bag) Bye Miss Roach.

Miss Roach

Bye Mrs Johnson.

Mo walks out of the classroom and waving to Billy, who's eating his dinner, she walks into the car park where Ron is waiting for her. She gets in the car.

Mo

(To Ron) You had to be there to believe it.

Everything Comes To Those Who Wait

Characters

Mo, Phoebe, Ron, Ben Hung, Vera Virus, Frigging Freda and Harold.

Setting

Mo's home and garden and the hairdressers.

Everything Comes To Those Who Wait

Mo is on the phone to Phoebe.

Mo

This is the third time you have phoned me in ten minutes. No, he has not arrived yet. Stop being so negative. Who wouldn't want to marry a sex crazed woman, twice his age. Yes I know Phoebe love, he should be very grateful for all the boots up the bum. I'm sure he will appreciate the fact that you have started to wear underwear because you want to be seen as a respectable woman, but at the end of the day, he still has not knocked on my door yet. Go and sit down and pour yourself a brandy. What do you mean you have had two already? It's nine o'clock in the morning. Right you alcoholic, I'll give you a ring if there's any news. I won't forget, bye Phoebe love, bye, bye. *(Mo put the phone down) (Talking to Ron)* Bloody hell, that woman's losing the plot. What am I going to do if he says no?

Ron

We will have to catch the first plane out to Australia.

Mo

She would still find us *(there is a knock at the door)* go and let him in.

Ron goes to the door and lets Ben in.

Ron

Hello Ben.

Ben Hung

Good morning Mr Johnson.

Ron

Call me Ron.

Ben Hung

Thank you Mr Johnson. *(He smiles)*

Ron

Mo is in the garden. (They both walk to the garden)

Mo

Good morning Ben.

Ben Hung

Good morning Mrs Johnson.

Mo

It's so nice of you to help Ron build his shed.

Ben Hung

My pleasure Mrs Johnson.

Ron

Right, I'll just finish my breakfast and we will make a start.

Ben Hung

Can I make a start now Mr Johnson?

Ron

Go on then. Everything you need is at the bottom of the garden.

Ben goes off to make a start.

Mo

Don't you just love his manners.

Ron

Yes Mrs Johnson. *(They both laugh)*

Mo

Any more of that and I'll be kicking you up the bum.

Ron

Yes Please Mrs Johnson. (*smiling*) Right I better give him a hand. *(Ron walks to the bottom of the garden)* Goodness me Ben, you're a quick worker. There's only the roof to be put. Another hour and we will be finished. *(They put the roof on and put the windows in)* Well done Ben. I thought it would take all day to do. Mo wants to get a greenhouse next. It would be great if you could help to put it up.

Ben Hung

I would be happy to help Mr Johnson. I've always wanted a greenhouse of my own. I enjoy growing things.

Ron

You will have to ask Phoebe.

Ben Hung

Mistress Phoebe prefers me doing jobs in the house and I don't want to upset her.

Ron

Mo is waving, it must be lunchtime. Come on. *(They both walk up the garden where Mo has laid out the table)*

Mo

Sit yourself down and help yourself Ben.

Ben Hung

Thank you Mrs Johnson.

Mo

Is there much more to do?

Ron

With Ben's speed and ability, we have finished.

Mo

Thank you Ben *(Ben smiles as he is eating)*

Ron

Ben is very happy to help putting up the greenhouse. He would like one of his own, to grow fruit and veg.

Mo

I'm sure we can sort that out for you.

After an hour, they have finished eating.

Ron

Who's doing the washing up?

Ben Hung

I will if you want Mrs Johnson?

Mo

No Ben, it's Ron's turn. Here, take the plates *(Ron takes the plates and goes into the kitchen)* Ben how are you getting on at Mrs Dickson's place?

Ben Hung

I love it Mrs Johnson. Mistress Phoebe is so kind to me. She let's me do all the jobs that need doing and lets me have a day working in the shop. As she always says why have a dog and bark yourself.

Mo

Does she. Where does this wanting to serve come from Ben?

Ben Hung

My father, Mrs Johnson.

Mo

Was he a strict father?

Ben Hung

Very strict Mrs Johnson, me and younger brother were given chores to do every day, but if we got the slightest thing wrong he would use the strap on us and tell us to start again. Sometimes we didn't get to bed till four in the morning.

Mo

What age were you Ben?

Ben Hung

It started when I was seven and my brother was five.

Mo

Did your mother help?

Ben Hung

She did as much as she could. But every time she intervened he would use the strap on her. Many times she would have a bust nose and a thick lip. He even broke her jaw once. She had to spend two weeks in hospital.

Mo

Did she never go to the police?

Ben Hung

Fear stopped her. She was petrified of him. There was always a chance that the police would let him go. He would have killed her.

Mo

How long did it go on for?

Ben Hung

Ten years Mrs Johnson.

Mo

Why did it stop?

Ben Hung

One day my brother missed the bus from school. So when he got home an hour later our father was waiting with his strap. As soon as he walked through the door, the beating started. My brother snapped and ran to the kitchen. He picked up a knife and stabbed him over ten times. An hour later the police took him away. Because of his age, he was detained at her majesty's pleasure in a young offenders jail. He was transferred to an adult prison when he became eighteen. He spent another eight years there until he was released on appeal. He lives down south now.

Mo

When was the last time you saw him?

Ben Hung

The last time was when the police took him away. He didn't want anyone to visit him inside. He always sends me a card on my birthday and at Christmas.

Mo

What happened to your mother?

Ben Hung

She blamed herself for what he did to us. Six months later she took an overdose. She was cremated on my eighteenth birthday. I stayed at a friend's mother's house who was very theatrical. She would do bits and bobs on television and that how I got into the business. But when you are told how worthless and useless you are, year after year, you start to believe it and expect people to treat you badly. But now I do feel at home. A place where I know I will never have to be subjected to the evil horrors, that happened before. *(He bursts out into tears. Mo holds him and kisses him on his cheek. After a couple of minutes, they sit down, holding hands)* Before you ask, I do want to marry her. I know she treats me like a dog's body, but not only do I enjoy it, but where as before I had no choice, now I do. I love her very much.

Mo
Thank goodness for that. I nearly threw the phone through the window.

Ben Hung
Can I ask her in your garden?

Mo
I'll give her a ring.*(Mo phones Phoebe)* Can you pop round? *(Seconds later, there is a banging on the door)* I wonder who that is. Right everyone, to your places. *(Ben Hung stands half way down the garden. Ben goes to the kitchen while Mo opens the door)* Can I help you madame?

Phoebe
Mo I can't stop shaking.

Mo
(In a formal voice) You will find Ben in the garden.

Phoebe walks into the garden to where Ben is standing.

Phoebe
If you don't want to marry me, that's fine, just don't leave me.

Mo
(Standing in the kitchen with Ron) Some dominatrix that one.

Ben Hung
(Going down on one knee and lifting up and engagement ring)
Will you marry me?

Phoebe
(With tears in her eyes) Yes, yes yes *(they both kiss)*

Mo and Ron walk to the garden table.

Mo
Champagne anyone? *(Walking up the garden, they all hug, holding their champagne glasses)* Congratulations Phoebe and Ben.

Phoebe
Mo I'm the happiest girl on the planet.

Mo
The ring looks beautiful.

Phoebe
Diamonds are a girl's best friend. After Ben of course.

Mo
When is the wedding to be?

Phoebe
As soon as possible I hope.

Mo
Leave it with me, I'll sort it.

Phoebe
You are a star Mo. Anyway we have to go as I have had to shut up the shop. If that bitch of an owner finds out, she will sack me. Come on Ben, we will do the shop together. *(Smiling, Ben and*

Phoebe walk out and wave down the path)

Mo

Right Ron, get the car out, I need to go to the hairdressers.

Ron

I thought you were there last week?

Mo

I was. It's to sort out this wedding.

Ron

Right, I'm on my way.

Mo

(Coming off the phone, she gets into the car) Let's get going.

Ron

Why is it always left to you to sort times?

Mo

We have been best friends for over forty years. There has been many times when she has been a godsend to me. Many times has she put food in my belly and money in my purse. She has been the bridesmaid too many times in her life.

Ron

I wish I had a best friend who could sort out my problems.

Mo

You have, it's me *(they both laugh)* right pull up. *(Mo gets out of the car and goes into the hairdressers)* Good afternoon everyone.

Vera Virus

Hello Mo, are you booked in?

Mo

No, I'm on a mission.

Frigging Freda

What's happened now?

Mo

Phoebe and Ben are getting married.

Frigging Freda

You could knock me down with a feather.

Vera Virus

I'm sorry Mrs Smith *(the lady having her hair done)* but I've got to sit down.

Frigging Freda

I thought it was business with those two.

Mo

Pleasure has taken over.

Vera Virus

I'm not surprised with his size.

Mo

I've phoned the church and the vicar said he has had a cancellation, three weeks on a Saturday at five o'clock.

Frigging Freda

How's that happened?

Mo

The bride to-be has gone lesbian, due to the fact her husband to-be was not well endowed. So I have booked the church Vera, she needs an outfit.

Vera Virus

I'm on the phone to Carol.

Mo

Freda can you sort the car and flowers?

Frigging Freda

Leave it with me, I'll sort it. *(Frigging Freda is on the phone)*

Vera Virus

(Talking on the phone) Carol are you sitting or standing? Phoebe and Ben are getting married, three weeks this Saturday. Carol love get Tony to pick you up off the floor and tell him to get you a brandy. Have you still got some of that white material? Not much. That must be because no-one stays a virgin these days before marriage. *(Everyone looks at Mo)*

Mo

Piss off.

Vera Virus

Carol love can you pop round in the morning? I'll see you then.

Harold walks through the door.

Harold

Well it sounded important when you left a message. What's up?

Mo

Phoebe and Ben are getting married, three weeks this Saturday.

Harold

Lucky cow. If I was getting married to Ben, I would get married naked. It would save time getting our clothes off.

Mo

You been watching 'Alice in Wonderland' again? Now can we have the reception in the Queens Head? The wedding is at five, so we will be there around six?

Harold

I'll see what I can do. But I will have to let the general public in at eight .

Mo

Two hours will give us enough time. What about entertainment?

Harold

There's Harold's wedding bingo and I'll find a couple of acts.

Mo

Don't bring out Rocky Rob. He's been dead too long.

Harold

How about asking Policeman Mickey to give us a couple of songs?

Mo

That's a good idea. Vera?

Vera Virus

Leave it with me, I'll have a word with Bella.

Mo

Don't forget to get a DJ and not the one you got last time. There's only so much garage music our generation can take. Also, can you ask Mini Meg, to see if her cooking class can make the cake and do the food.

Harold

Well I don't know about Alice, but with all this to do, the hole

I'm falling down is a black hole.

Vera Virus
Well it will match your own. After all that never sees the light of day either.

Harold
I don't know what you mean? *(They all laugh)*

Mo
Before I forget, it's Phoebe's hen night next Friday. Make sure you are all available.

Vera Virus
What about the something old, something new? Should I do better?

Mo
We should do really.

Vera Virus
Well the something old, she is bringing herself. The something new is her husband, as it's all new to her with the size of his penis. The something borrowed, she has done that with everyone in the village and never gave anything back. The something blue is the veins in her legs. *(Everyone laughs)*

Mo
Thank you Vera, we will talk about it later. Right I'm off. I'll see you all later.

All
Bye Mo.

She walks out of the hairdressers and into the car, kissing Ron on the cheek.

Mo

That's all sorted.

A Night To Remember

Characters

Dilys and Philys

Two small ladies in their eighties. They have been friends for many years.

Lucky Legs Linda

A tall woman in her late twenties. She has a reputation of enjoying the company of men.

Other Characters

Mo, Phoebe, Carol, Pill Gill, Mini Meg, Vera Virus, Frigging Freda, Brenda Shield Ore, The Fella Bella, Penny Pick a Nose, Mr M, Ron, Tony, Dick, Ben Hung, Harold, Jack and the young Bowager.

Settings

Mo's cottage, in the taxi, Laughing Cow, Queen's Head.

A Night To Remember

Phoebe knocks on Mo's door.

Mo

(Shouting from the kitchen) Come in and sit on the sofa.

Phoebe

What the hell is going on?

Mo

(From the kitchen) For one night only, singers from each decade of your life have assembled to sing for you tonight.

Frigging Freda

Tonight Matthew, I'm going to be Cliff Richard. *(Dressed as Cliff Richard, Frigging Freda mimes to 'Devil Woman' which is playing on a CD player)*

Phoebe

Freda you are a star.

Vera Virus

Tonight Matthew, I'm going to be Elvis Presley. *(Dressed as Elvis, she sings 'You Ain't Nothing But A Hound Dog')*

Phoebe

Wonderful Vera.

Mo

Now we move to the 1960s, a decade Phoebe remembers very little of. *(laughing)*

Mini Meg
Tonight Matthew, I'm going to be Paul McCartney of the Beatles. *(Dressed as Paul McCartney, she mimes to 'Help')*

Phoebe
Brilliant Meg.

Stella
Tonight Matthew, I'm going to be Tammy Wynette. *(She mimes to 'Stand By Your Man)*

Phoebe
(Hugging Stella) Thank you Stella love. You look amazing.

Mo
Now we move to the seventies. Another decade Phoebe doesn't remember much about. *(They all laugh)*

Carol
Tonight Matthew, I'm going to be Donny Osmond. *(Dressed as Donny Osmond, she mimes to 'And They Call It, Puppy Love')*

Phoebe
Super Carol.

Mo
Tonight Matthew, I'm going to be Frida Applegren from ABBA *(she sings 'Knowing Me, Knowing You')*

Phoebe
You are a star. *(They hug)*

Going back into the kitchen, she picks up the microphone.

Mo
Now we move to the eighties. Not surprisingly, you can still buy

tins of soup from this decade in Phoebe's shop today. *(They all laugh)*

Phoebe

I don't know what you mean.

Janice

Tonight Matthew, I'm going to be Michael Jackson. *(She sings 'Thriller.' Everyone gets up to do the dance moves)*

Phoebe

Marvellous Janice.

Pill Gill

Tonight Matthew, I'm going to be 'George Michael' of Wham. *(She mimes to 'Wake Me Up, Before You Go Go')*

Phoebe

Mistress Wonders, you can thrash out a song.

Mo

Ladies and Ladies, we now move to the nineties, where Phoebe still doesn't know what a bra is. *(Everyone laughs)*

Sheila Ore

Tonight Matthew, I'm going to be Madonna. *(She mimes to 'Like a Virgin.' Everyone is rolling around laughing)*

Phoebe

That was brilliant Sheila. An honest performance.

Brenda

Tonight Matthew, I'm going to be 'Britney Spears.' *(Dressed in thigh high length boots and a short skirt, Brenda mimes to 'Baby One More Time')*

Vera Virus

It's a good job she was wearing knickers.

Phoebe

A star is born.

Penny Pick a Nose

Tonight Matthew, I'm going to be 'Pink.' *(With pink hair, she mimes to 'You Make Me Sick')*

Carol

That's a colour she is not familiar with.

Frigging Freda

What's the song called?

Vera Virus

'You Make Me Sick.'

Frigging Freda

Does Pink eat cake as well? *(Everyone falls about laughing)*

Phoebe

Penny that was wonderful. Those plasters on your fingers really make it look authentic.

The Fella Bella

Tonight Matthew, I'm going to be 'Beyonce Knowles.' *(Dressed in the tightest outfit, The Fella Bella mimes to 'Crazy in Love')*

Phoebe

You were wonderful.

Mo

On behalf of our Phoebe, I would like to thank Vera and Carol for the costumes and to the wonderful Bella for sorting out the music and make-up. (*Everyone claps*) Right ladies, it's time to party. The taxis are here.

Everyone walks out, where they put a veil on Phoebe's head and a big sticker on her back saying 'Bride to be.'

Vera Virus

Come on girls. (*Everyone gets into the taxi*)

Mo gets in to the front of the first taxi with Carol, Phoebe and Janice in the back.

Carol

(*Shouting out of the window*) Meg get yourself in here, you can sit on my knee. (*Meg does this*)

Taxi Driver

It's not every day I get Paul McCartney, ABBA, Donny Osmond and Michael Jackson in my cab at the same time.

Mo

All Paul would sing 'Let it be, Let it be'. (*They all start singing the song*)

Carol

(*Getting a bottle of vodka out of her bag*) Anyone for a drink?

Mo

Carol what are you like.

Carol

You only get married once. (*They all look at Mo, even the taxi driver*)

Mo

Sod off.

They all take a couple of swigs from the bottle.

Janice

(Getting a bottle of pink gin out of her bag) Anyone for a drink?

Mo

I can't believe this.

Janice

So you don't want any?

Mo

Are you having a laugh, pass it here. *(They all laugh)*

Mini Meg

If you can't beat them, join them *(she pulls out a bottle of Malibu. Everyone cheers).*

Taxi Driver

It's a good job we have arrived. With all these fumes, I would be pulled over for drink driving and I haven't touched a drop.

They all get out and sway over to the door of the Laughing Cow.

Bouncer

Sorry ladies not tonight. You have had enough.

Carol

Girls, he thinks we have had enough.

Phoebe

We have, of him. Everyone charge. *(They all charge forward, knocking the bouncer over)*

Mo

Girls *(they all face Mo)* 'The winner takes it all' *(they all join in)*

Jack

(The other bouncer) What's going on out here?

Mo

Now there's a bit of quality.

Jack

Hello Mrs Johnson. *(They both hug)*

Mo

How's that gorgeous child of yours?

Jack

He's doing great. Thank you so much.

Mo

You are very welcome. Sorry about your mate.

Jack

It's his first night.

Mo

You never forget your first night.

Jack

He certainly won't *(they both laugh)* you have a great night.

Stepping over the bouncer, Mo walks into the pub and over to the bar.

Vera Virus

Don't order a drink Mo, that young looking guy sitting over there has just brought you a double.

Mo sees Mr M waving at her. She walks over to him.

Mr M

Hello you wonderful lady. *(They hug)*

Mo

So why are you out tonight?

Mr M

It's Woody's birthday, although he's been in the toilet for the last half hour. I wouldn't be surprised if Sheila Ore, the black widow spider has got her fangs into him. Although if she gets his bits to rise it will be a miracle. So why are you out?

Mo

You see that drunken tart over there?

Mr M

Mutton dressed as a lamb.

Mo

That's her. Well she is getting married in a couple of weeks and the bloke she is marrying always gets his bits to rise. But there again he is half her age.

Mr M

Well, it's certainly keeping her fit.

Mo

She works out most days. *(They both laugh)* How's that little boy doing?

Mr M

Who, Gary?

Mo

That's him.

Mr M

He's just hanging on with everything that's happened. You know the father was arrested and put on remand.

Mo

No.

Mr M

While he was inside, two of the other prisoners walked into his cell and stabbed him. He died two days later.

Mo

Would you believe it.

Mr M

It seems these days we have to rely on other prisoners to get justice. Let the people vote for the death penalty. In my eyes, the fear of being hanged will stop our children being murdered.

Mo

What about the mother?

Mr M

I'm afraid drugs and drink have taken over her life. She walked out leaving him with no food. If a neighbour hadn't heard his cries for help, who knows what might have happened. He's in foster care now. But being as she looks after other children as well, Gary doesn't get the attention he deserves to bring him out of the depression he's going through. I do go and visit him every Saturday, but he really needs to be adopted by a couple who doesn't have children, so he can get the attention he needs.

Mo

Can you do me a favour?

Mr M

Of course.

Mo

Can you bring Gary to my place next Saturday, there's someone I want him to meet. Two o'clock alright?

Mr M

I'll see you then.

Mo

Right, my lot are waving me over. I'll see you next Saturday.

Mo walks over to the dance floor with the rest of the girls. After ten minutes, the music stops and the announcer comes on stage.

Announcer

Ladies and Gentlemen, just flown in from Las Vegas.

The Fella Bella

Don't you mean, just flown in from my bedroom? *(Everyone laughs)*

Announcer

For one night only, the fabulous, the amazing Isla Bligh *(Policeman Mickey comes onto the stage in drag)*

Policeman Mickey

Well, we have got some hot babes in here tonight and what's this? One of them is getting married. Come up and see me Miss Dickson. *(Phoebe goes onto the stage)* Well guys, look at the one you allowed to get away.

Phoebe

Stop it.

Policeman Mickey

That's the first time I've ever heard you say that. Now I see you have bought some celebrities with you. I think we should see the sort of people you are hanging out with. Hearing about your husband to be, hanging out describes him well. Even Tarzan could swing from one side of the jungle to the other on that size. I thought you were walking bow legged because you were pissed. Well lets get them up on stage. *(Policeman Mickey shouts each of the celebrities names out and they walk on the stage to the sound of cheering)* Well that's a sight you don't see very often. Looking down the line I can see, not only a hot beauty I'm getting married to next year, but a wonderful group. Play the music. *(Policeman Mickey starts to sing 'Dancing Queen' and everyone starts to dance)*

After the song, they all go to the bar and order a drink.

Mo

This will have to be the last one here. The men are waiting for us at the Queens Head.

Phoebe

Is that Pissy Pete who always has a leak?

Mo

Looking at his soaking wet trousers, it must be.

Vera Virus

You know why that is don't you?

Mo

No.

Vera Virus

Every time he goes to the toilet, which is about every ten minutes, Sheila Ore presses a button, which locks all the toilets except for hers. What does a young good looking lad do? Use an old woman's toilet or wet himself?

Phoebe

If it was me I would be soaked from head to toe.

Mo

Do you remember when he got married, the bride had to buy two wedding dresses, which was a good job she did. After their first dance together, the bride looked like a drowned rat.

Phoebe

Is she still with him?

Mo

No, she got fed up of sleeping on a piss soaked bed. She is with a lifeguard now.

Phoebe

Not everyone likes those water beds.

Mo

Right, come on everyone, taxi's here.

They all stumble out into the taxis. Twenty minutes later, they are outside the Queen's Head. They all burst through the door doing the conga.

Harold

Bloody hell, here they go. 'Legs and co'. *(They are all dancing to 'Give Me, Give Me, Give Me' when there is a scream)*

Lucky Legs Linda

My waters have broken. The baby is coming!

Mo

Someone phone for an ambulance. Lie her on the pool table. *(Ron, Dick, Tony and Ben Hung all lift her)* Careful *(Lucky Legs Linda screams out)* Phoebe, take her knickers off and push her skirt up. *(Phoebe does this)*

Phoebe

I love your knickers Linda, where did you get them from?

Mo

Not now Phoebe love. Harold, get me some hot water and towels.

Mini Meg

Let's have a look how dilated she is. Tony bring me a box to stand on. *(Tony brings a box over)* Tony, I want to see her vagina not her big toe!

Carol

You stupid man, go and get that big box in the corner. This is what I have to put up with. Don't you know...

Mo

Not now Carol love.

Tony brings the box over and lifts Meg onto it.

Mini Meg

The head is right down. Give it a few minutes before she starts pushing.

Carol

If any man comes near this pool table, I'll sit on them. *(All the men back away)*

Dilys and Philys walk over to the pool table with their knitting.

Philys

Dilys, have you felt this young woman's legs? They are beautifully smooth..

Dilys

They are Philys. *(Both woman are stroking Lucky Leg Linda's legs)* Do you think she uses Immac or Veet?

Philys

I think she has had them waxed.

Dilys

You know, you could be right. *(Both woman sit at the opposite end of the pool table and start doing their knitting)* Talking of wax, I think she has had one of them Brazilians on her front bottom.

Philys

Wait a minute, let me get my glasses *(she searches in her bag and finds her glasses, putting them on)* I think you're right Dilys. They have done a very good job. Everything looks so neat and tidy.

Dilys

I've had a Brazilian before you know.

Philys

Have you? When was that?

Dilys

Last Christmas. Mavis brought me a box of Brazil nuts.

Philys

Did she. All I got was a bar of Cadbury's whole nut.

Dilys

The tight bitch. What did we buy her?

Philys

We didn't, due to the fact she needs to go on a diet.

Dilys

That was very thoughtful of you.

Philys

I say Dilys, I see she paints her toenails.

Dilys

So she does. But I'm not mad about that colour.

Philys

I know what you mean.

Dilys

I went to a friend's house once and had to use her bathroom.

Philys

What colour was it?

Dilys

Avocado.

Philys

That's a shame.

Dilys

It was. The colour messed up all of my functions.

Philys

How was that?

Dilys

Well I went for a wee, but my bottom felt compelled to interrupt.

Philys

That was inconvenient.

Dilys

Not as much as I had to use a towel because she had ran out of toilet paper.

Philys

That's shocking Dilys.

Dilys

It was. Mind you she died soon after.

Philys

How did she die?

Dilys

She crashed her car into the sewage works.

Philys

That's terrible.

Dilys

The car burst into flames.

Philys

She died shit hot then?

Dilys

She was always a good looking woman.

Philys

Mo love, there's movement in the front bottom.

Mini Meg

Right Linda push. *(After a few pushes, the babies head pops out)*

Dilys

Did you see that Philys?

Philys

See what?

Dilys

That baby just winked at me.

Philys

It's definitely a boy then.

Mini Meg

Now one more big push and he will be out. *(She screams as she pushes him out)* The baby is out. *(Picking up the baby)* You have a beautiful baby boy. *(Mini Meg gives the baby to Mo, who gives it to Lucky Legs Linda)*

Mo

He is beautiful. Any ideas of names?

Lucky Legs Linda

I want to name him after the people who helped deliver him. I'm going to call him Paul Donny Elvis Cliff.

Mo

That's wonderful.

Harold
(Passing out glasses of Champagne) Raise your glasses, to mother and child.

Everyone
Mother and child.

Everyone starts to sing 'Let It Be' as the blue lights of the ambulance are flashing through the windows.

Where One Life Is Closing, Another Is Beginning

Characters

Gary

A five year old boy, who has seen a lot of physical abuse from his stepfather, leaving him timid and withdrawn.

Peterson

A medium sized man in his sixties. He has worked at the Manor for over forty years, twenty of them as the butler.

Other Characters

Mo, Phoebe, Ben Hung, Ron, Mr M and the Duke.

Setting

The Manor House, Mo's cottage.

Where One Life Is Closing, Another Is Beginning

Mo has just come off the phone, looking pale.

Ron

Are you alright?

Mo

Not really.

Ron

Who was it on the phone?

Mo

It was the Manor. The Duke wants to see me.

Ron

I thought he hated you?

Mo

He does.

Ron

Well, if he hates you, why does he want to see you?

Mo

Does it look at though I've got a crystal ball?

Ron

I'm just saying.

Mo

Well don't.

Ron

Fine. *(He walks out into the garden)*

Mo goes upstairs and changes her clothes. She is seen walking up the lane towards the Manor. As she approaches, the Manor gates open. She walks through them and up to the house. She rings the bell. Peterson the butler opens the door.

Peterson

Good morning Mrs Johnson.

Mo

Good morning Peterson.

Peterson

The Duke is expecting you.

The butler leads Mo upstairs to the Duke's bedroom. The butler knocks and walks into the bedroom.

Peterson

Mrs Johnson, Your Grace.

Leading Mo into the bedroom, Peterson leaves and shuts the door. Mo can see all the curtains have been drawn, with several candles lighting the room.

The Duke

(Staring into Mo's face) I can see you are surprised to be here Mrs Johnson.

Mo

Shocked would be a better word.

The Duke

I'm sure you are.

Mo

Why am I here?

The Duke

I wanted to see the thing I hate and despise for one last time.

Mo

Strong words, Your Grace.

The Duke

For what you did to my mother, they should be stronger. Words like whore and slut would be better.

Mo

Is that right Your Grace. Well, if it wasn't for this whore you hate so much, you wouldn't be laying in that bed, acting like an arrogant twat.

The Duke

You vile bitch. How dare you say the woman who gave me so much love is not my mother.

Mo

She is not.

The Duke

Then who is?

Mo

Me.

The Duke

You lying slut.

Mo

The woman you knew as your mother had pregnancy after pregnancy, but she lost every one of them. It was that, which made her weak and brought her to an ugly death.

The Duke
Liar.

Mo
It is no lie Your Grace. The boy you shared an upbringing with is your twin brother, who was born first. So it is he who should now be the Duke. Even the woman you call your sister was born by one of your father's mistresses, and if you don't believe me speak to your aunt, she is the only other person who knows about what happened.

The Duke
(*Shouting*) Get out you piece of trash!

Mo
Goodbye Your Grace. I hope your death will be better than your miserable life.

The Duke
(*Shouting*) Whore!

Mo opens the door and when closing it, she takes a deep breath, wiping away her tears.

Peterson
Is everything alright Mrs Johnson?

Mo
It is now.

Peterson
I'll lead you out Mrs Johnson. (*As they are walking out*)

Mo

You have been here a long time, have you not?

Peterson

Over forty-years Mrs Johnson. But with things the way they are, I think it's time I left.

Mo

Hold out a little longer, the next Duke will need a fine butler like yourself. Goodbye Peterson.

Peterson

Goodbye Mrs Johnson.

Mo walks through the door and up to the gates. She looks back and smiles. Ten minutes later, Mo walks up her garden path. Ron opens up the door and Mo walks into Ron's open arms.

Mo

I'm sorry for being so grumpy.

Ron

Well, as long as you're not grumpy in the bedroom. *(He picks her up and as they climb the stairs, there is a knock on the door)* Ignore it, they will go away.

Mo

As I know who it is, there isn't a chance they will go away. Now put me down Prince Charming and go and put the kettle on.

Ron

Yes me lady.

Mo opens the door.

Phoebe

There better be a good reason for you insisting that I come round. We are supposed to be shopping for shoes and bags.

Mo

Good afternoon Mrs Dickson, it's so nice to see you too. *(Phoebe and Ben Hung walk into the living room)*

Phoebe

Now what's all this about?

Mo

I've invited you both round to meet a very special person.

Phoebe

Don't tell me 'Pissed up Pete who likes it neat' wants a pre-wedding chat?

Mo

He only meets people when the offie is shut. There is someone I want you both to meet.

Phoebe

You are definitely up to something Maureen Johnson.

There is a knock on the door. Mo goes to answer it.

Mr M

Hello you beautiful lady.

Mo

Good afternoon Mr M. Good afternoon Gary.

Gary

Hello Mrs Johnson.

Mo

Come in *(they walk into the living room)* This is Mr & Mrs Clarkson.

Gary

(Putting his hand out) Hello Mrs Clarkson. You wear beautiful clothes.

Phoebe

A boy who knows quality when he sees it.

Ben

Hello. I'm Ben. What's your name?

Gary

My name is Gary, and I'm five years old. But in ten days time I'm going to be six.

Ben

Do you know Gary, Mrs Johnson has a beautiful garden, shall we go and have a look at it?

Gary

Yes please Ben.

Ben

Come on then. *(They both walk out into the garden)*

Mo

This is Mr M, that wonderful teacher I was telling you about.

Phoebe

Hello Mr M.

Mr M

Hello you fine lady.

Phoebe

You are too kind.

Mr M

Would you mind if I popped out for an hour? Mr Browny has got himself in a bit of trouble.

Mo

Not at all, what's he done?

Mr M

Well, you know the last time we were all at the Laughing Cow?

Mo

Yes.

Mr M

Well, so was Miss Lovelace. Each drink Mr Browny had made Miss Lovelace look a bit better, to the point where he thought she looked like a model.

Mo

Did he drink the bar dry?

Mr M

And every other bar too. Anyway, to cut a long story short, he woke up to her daughter saying, "Is this my new daddy?" But even worse, Miss Lovelace said, "This is your new daddy, and he has helped mummy to make a new brother or sister for you."

Mo

Nightmare. Get yourself off Mr M, I'll see you in a bit. *(Mr M takes his leave)*

Phoebe

I know what your game is now.

Mo

Now before you kick off. How many times have you told me that Ben has always wanted to have children? I know you can still breast feed, but you have reached your sell by date, just like half the items in your shop.

Phoebe

I don't know what you mean. *(They both laugh)*

Mo

He is a five year-old boy who has been through a terrible time and needs people in his life who will love him.

Phoebe

But don't you think Mo, at my time of life, should I be taking on a five year old boy? My name is not Elizabeth and I'm not having a son called John.

Mo

If he was to baptise you, the holy water would soon turn to wine.

Phoebe

Are you trying to say I would be an unfit mother?

Mo

You would be a wonderful mother in name.

Phoebe

But it's Ben I'm worried about.

Mo

Are you?

Phoebe

I am. With all the jobs he has to do each day, then there's the shop and my needs. You think Mo, he is going to have to take him to school each day and pick him up. He is going to have more washing and ironing to do. There is going to be another mouth to feed, so there will be more cooking and shopping to do. Someone has to think of these things.

Mo

Of course you will be there to lend a hand.

Phoebe

Well, I could read him a bed night story a couple of times a week.

Mo

(*Sarcastically*) That shows you what a wonderful mother you will be. You do want to make Ben happy don't you?

Phoebe

I do Mo. Although I will have to be quieter in the bedroom.

Mo

Well get Ben to put his hand over your mother. It will be like sado-masochism role play.

Phoebe

I never thought of that.

Mr M knocks at the door. Mo goes to answer it.

Mo

Come in Mr M. How's Mr Browny doing?

Mr M

Not well. He's in deep shock. There are beer bottles all over the place. Charlie, the year six boy, is round Mr Browny's house every five minutes selling him fags. His mother will be able to go on a cruise around the world with the amount he's making.

Ben and Gary come in from the garden.

Mo

Hello you two.

Ben

We have had a really good time.

Gary

It's been great. Do you know Mr M, Ben said we can go to the church next week to see him get married.

Mr M

That's really kind of him. We better get you back. Say goodbye to everyone. *(Gary says his goodbyes and as he is walking out, he runs back to give Ben a big hug)*

Ben

I'll see you next week. *(Ben walks with Gary to the door and waves him off)*

Phoebe

Right, we better go while the shops are still open.

Phoebe kisses Mo, and as they walk down the lane, Ben runs back with a tear in his eye and gives Mo a big hug. Ron comes out from the kitchen.

Ron

Have they all gone?

Mo

They have for now.

Ron

You really are a saint Mrs Johnson. You need to be elevated to a higher place.

Mo

(With a smile) I don't know what you mean Mr Johnson.

Ron

Do you not? Let me show you.

Ron picks up Mo and carries her upstairs.

The Big Day

Characters

Simon

He is of medium height with a very friendly personality. He is a couple of years younger than his brother, Ben Hung. He is very open minded when it comes to his sexuality.

Other Characters

Mo, Phoebe, Ben Hung, Ron, Vera Virus and Bert, Carol and Tony, Frigging Freda, Jancie, Harold, Policeman Mickey and the Fella Bella, Mini Meg, Penny Pick a Nose and Pissed up Pete who likes it neat.

Setting

Mo's cottage, the church, The Queen's Head.

Self Reflection

The Big Day

Mo is in the kitchen with Ron.

Mo

Do you know, if that woman bangs on the bedroom floor again, I'm going to slap her.

Ron

Now it's her big day, so she is bound to feel a bit needy.

Mo

Needy! She will need an ambulance if she carries on. This will be her third cup of tea in an hour and she didn't wake up till ten.

Ron

(Passing Mo the tray) I've done her a full English.

Mo

It's eleven o'clock.

Ron

You have had a full English much later than this. Now that's food for thought.

Mo

It would be if you were talking about food, *(they both laugh)* I'm in a good mind to shove those sausages where the sun don't shine.

Ron

It's her big day.

Mo

And it will be her last day if she carries on.

Mo goes upstairs to the spare bedroom. She opens the door.

Phoebe

I thought you had emigrated?

Mo

Do you want to eat this breakfast or wear it?

Phoebe

You are kind to let me stay at yours for the night. You wouldn't want the groom to see the bride until she is walking down the aisle in virgin white.

Mo

With your reputation, you should be walking down the aisle in deepest black.

Phoebe

How dare you Mrs Johnson, and me to be with child soon.

Mo

Are we talking about Gary or your husband to be?

Phoebe

Wash your mouth out woman. But on a serious note, do you think I'm doing the right thing?

Mo

What, by getting married?

Phoebe

No, but letting him adopt a child.

Mo

Knowing how much Gary means to him, I think you will find if it's a toss up between Gary or yourself, you will be back doing the house work and buying some new batteries for your 'rampant rabbit'.

Phoebe
Then I was right to let him adopt. I just hope with all his jobs he has to do he will manage the child too.

Mo
You could always give him a hand?

Phoebe
This is a lovely breakfast, where did you get this bacon from?

Mo
Johnny Bates farm.

Phoebe
Not farmer Johnny who loves his mummy?

Mo
I've always found him to be very helpful.

Phoebe
That's what his ex-girlfriend was hoping for. But every time he was at his peak in the bedroom, his mother could be heard shouting his name to come and give her a hand.

Mo
That's not good.

Phoebe
This went on for weeks, until the girlfriend couldn't take it any more. She even got Johnny to buy more carrots, but nothing worked. The thought of having a son that would be known as Master Bates was the last straw. But do you know Mo, she would never use the shower.

Mo

So the moral of the story is?

Phoebe

To answer those who say 'are you doing the right thing?' What's the point of being able to see in the dark if there is no piece of young meat to find. How many woman of our age turn the carrots into themselves?

Mo

Right, I want you downstairs in half a hour. Carol and Vera will be here within the hour.

Phoebe

I don't know why they are coming so early?

Mo

(Picking up a mirror) Does that tell you why?

Phoebe

How dare you. At least I'm getting married in daylight, unlike some who prefer the darkest to make themselves feel comfortable.

Mo

Carry on lady and it will be my first night funeral. It will be interesting to see the witches taking away your spirit.

Phoebe

Talking about spirits, do you think it's too early to have a brandy to calm my nerves?

Mo

You have got half a hour to get yourself down those stairs. *(Mo leaves the bedroom)*

Thirty minutes later, Phoebe descends the stairs with her tray.

Ron

Let me take that off you young lady.

Phoebe

You are a star Ron. You are so the right man to give me away. But as you see Ron my nerves are all over the place. You couldn't get me a brandy, while the wicked witch of the west isn't around?

Ron

Leave it with me. You will find Mo in the garden.

Phoebe

You are a wonderful man. *(Phoebe walks into the garden and sits down next to Mo)*

Mo

You made it then?

Phoebe

Hello Mo. Do you know Mo, it's been over forty years that our friendship has lasted. The favours we have done for each other over the years. Do you remember we went out dancing with those two guys who had travelled down from Scotland. As we were dancing around our handbags, you tripped over the strap. Mind you, you made sure you had finished your gin and tonic as the ambulance men took you to hospital.

Mo

You didn't get in the ambulance with me, if I remember rightly.

Phoebe

Well, I wanted to. But the guys had just got another round in and they had travelled all the way to see me.

Mo

Slut.

Phoebe

But like the true friend I was, I came to visit you in hospital the next day and gave you all the details of the night before.

Mo

That was kind of you.

Phoebe

Do you also remember, we got off with the farmer's sons in one of their fields that time?

Mo

They weren't very well endowed as I remember.

Phoebe

You're right they weren't. But they were only nineteen, so we didn't have the heart to tell them to stop. It was a good job the bull came along when it did.

Mo

Don't mention that bull.

Phoebe

It's not every night you see two naked woman running across the field with a bull after them.

Mo

It wasn't so bad for you, you jumped the fence the first time. I got caught on the top bar. I can still feel that bulls tongue on my bottom today.

Phoebe

What ever happened to that bull?

Mo

Well every morning I had to walk past that field on the way to work and the bull would come running towards me with its tongue out.

Phoebe

Nightmare.

Mo

But a few weeks later, it was gone.

Phoebe

Where did it go?

Mo

I heard he couldn't perform his duties to the cows because he had tasted human flesh, so they got rid of it.

Phoebe

So you could say, he went from having it with an animal cow, to having it with a human cow. *(They both burst out laughing)*

Ron

Your drinks me ladies.

Mo

I can't drink brandy at this time of the day.

Phoebe

Bullshit. *(They both burst out laughing)*

There is a loud knock at the door.

Mo

Here they are. Ron go and let them in and pour a couple more brandies.

Ron opens the door.

Carol

Hi Ron *(she gives Ron a hug)*

Vera Virus

Hi Ron *(she gives him a kiss on the cheek)*

Ron

You will find them both in the garden.

They both dance into the garden singing 'Phoebe's getting married to her Benny, ding dong the bells are going to chime, he's got a whopper and Phoebe loves his chopper, so get her to the church on time.' They all fall about laughing.

Mo

You daft pair, get yourselves sat down.

Ron brings them a brandy each.

Carol

You are a star.

Vera Virus

This is a nice bit of brandy Mo, which shop did you get it from?

Mo

Don't ask me, one of the children's mum's gets it knocked off.

Vera Virus

Order me a couple of bottles Mo, it's good stuff.

Carol

I'll have two bottles as well.

Vera Virus

Mo, you smell lovely, what is that?

Mo

It's Prada Woman.

Vera Virus

What shop did you get that from?

Mo

Don't ask me. Another of the children's mum's get it knocked off. She sells them for a tenner.

Carol

Bloody hell, I don't know about Saint Mo, more like Ma Baker. Does she sell any more?

Mo

She has got 'Lady Millions' as well.

Carol

(Pulling out twenty pounds from her purse) Get me one of each.

Vera Virus

The same for me.

Phoebe

Me too.

Mo

One thing I'll say about you lot, you never take the moral high ground.

Carol

We gave that up when we married. Let's face it girls, we could rewrite the Kamasutra and call it 'A woman's position in the home.'

Mo

Well, Phoebe wouldn't contribute much to that book.

Phoebe

What do you mean?

Mo

All you do is lie down on the sofa eating peeled grapes.

Phoebe

I'll have you know my Ben has not got the time to peel my grapes. That's why I prefer them quashed, so I can drink them. *(They all laugh)*

Mo

Right young lady, it's time you got in that bath.

Vera Virus

It's going to take me a few hours to sort out that face, so don't be too long.

Carol

I would have thought days myself.

Phoebe

Piss off you two. *(Phoebe goes upstairs to the bathroom)*

Vera Virus

Who would have thought we would be sitting here drinking brandy on a Saturday afternoon because Phoebe Dickson is getting married.

Carol

Do you think it's a love job?

Mo

Definitely. She loves to see him do all the jobs. But there again, if the man you are with makes you happy, then it doesn't matter what age you get married. I'm living proof of that.

Carol

Talking of proof, any chance of getting the same, seventy percent proof again?

Mo

(*Shouting*) Ron you gorgeous man, any chance of another drink?

Ron

(*Carrying a tray of brandies*) Your wish is my command me lady. (*He kisses Mo on the cheek as he walks back into the kitchen*)

Carol

You will never guess who I saw in the supermarket the other day?

Vera Virus

Who?

Carol

Nightmare Dave who needs an early grave.

Vera Virus

Not that nasty, vile bloke who has never got a good word to say about anyone.

Carol

That's the one. Well, anyway, I parked my car the same time as he did. A Romanian car washer bloke came up to Nightmare Dave and said, "Car wash sir?" and Nightmare Dave said, "Do you understand any English?" The Romanian said, "A little." and Nightmare Dave replied, "Good. Then you will understand the words piss off."

Vera Virus

Nasty man.

Carol

It gets better. So getting his trolley he starts going up and down the aisles until he gets to the top of the third aisle, where he can see that an old woman has collapsed on the floor. Nightmare Dave says to the woman standing next to her, "What's her problem then? Has she been on the vodka or is she just after attention?" Well, the woman, open-mouthed, couldn't believe what she was hearing. Next minute, Nightmare Dave walks down the aisle, just as the doctor puts a blanket over the dead woman's head, and says out loud "Why did she have to die next to the tinned peas? I'll have to think of something else to go with my pie now."

Mo

There's a guy going to hell.

Carol

Next minute he goes to the cake section and says to the woman behind the counter, "I'm looking for a nice bit of cake, what would you recommend, seeing as you must have tried them all with your weight problem."

Mo

No.

Carol

There's more. Nightmare Dave picked up a loaf of bread and checked the sell by date. Next minute he kept saying to the assistant excuse me, but unknown to him the woman is wearing a hearing aid, which she had forgotten to switch on. So every time Nightmare Dave is saying excuse me, the assistant just smiles and nods. In the end Nightmare Dave says, 'it's like talking to the living dead' and that he's seen more life in a tramp's vest.

Vera Virus

Nasty man.

Carol

The icing on the cake was, he got a lottery ticket and got five balls and the bonus.

Mo

It seems the nastier and greedier you are, the more life seems to reward you.

There is a knock on the door. Ron goes to open it.

Tommy/Jenny

Hello Uncle Ron.

Ron

Hello you two. *(They rush into the cottage and head for the garden, shouting Aunty Mo)*

Mo

(Hugging each other) Hello you two. Where's your mother?

Tommy

Mummy is hugging Uncle Ron.

Mo

What that woman does to get a drink.

Carol

It's less than what you have to do.

Mo

You're right, but there again. I'm doing it for the bottle. *(They all laugh)*

Jenny

Aunty Carol, have you made me a beautiful dress?

Carol
(Hugging Jenny) A beautiful dress for a beautiful princess.

Tommy
Aunty Vera.

Vera Virus
Yes my darling?

Tommy
My hair keeps sticking up.

Vera Virus
Would you like your Aunty Vera to have a look at it?

Tommy
Yes please.

Brenda walks into the garden with a brandy.

Mo
Fancy a mother of two drinking brandy in the afternoon.

Brenda
(Hugging Mo) With these two running me ragged, I'm surprised I haven't hit the bottle.

Mo
Where's your husband?

Brenda
Wait for it, he's got man flu.

Carol
Not that old chestnut.

Brenda

But he thinks he will make the Queens Head by six.

Carol

My Tony said that once. He made the bottom of the stairs at six, after I had pushed him down them. His flu soon flew away. *(Everyone laughs)*

Vera Virus

Right Carol, let's sort these two out before Queen Cleopatra descends on us.

Brenda

Where is she?

Mo

Last heard she was bathing in asses milk.

Carol

I don't know about bathing in it, but her ass needs a good kick.

After half a hour, the children are ready and Phoebe, in a dressing gown, with a towel on her head, descends the stairs.

Mo

Here comes the Queen of Sheba.

Phoebe

Hello everyone and thank you for coming to my wedding.

Vera Virus

You don't hear that everyday.

Carol

With Phoebe Dickson, you don't expect to hear it any day.

Vera Virus
Phoebe Dickson, if I don't make a start on your face now, you will be going up the aisle looking like the bride of Frankenstein. *(Vera Virus makes a start on Phoebe's hair and face)*

Billy comes through the door.

Mo
Where have you been?

Billy
We had a last minute rush, where dad put everything at half price.

Mo
Now you have another last minute rush to get yourself in that shower and dressed, now move. *(As he rushes up the stairs, Mo shouts him back. Billy comes back downstairs)*

Billy
What?

Mo
Give your brother and sister a hug and tell them how wonderful they look.

Billy
(Hugging them both) You both look wonderful.

Mo
Aunty Brenda needs a hug.

Brenda
Hello darling.

Mo
Aunty Carol needs a hug.

Carol
Hello darling.

Mo
Give Aunt Vera a hug.

Vera Virus
Hello you wonderful boy.
(After hugging everyone)

Mo
Right, now move it. *(Billy moves towards Mo and gives her a deep hug, then runs upstairs)*

Carol
Now that is the sort of hug that melts your heart.

Brenda
The taxi is here.

Mo
Brenda, take your two and tell the taxi to come back.

Brenda
I will do. *(They leave and get into the taxi)*

Mo
How's she looking Vera?

Vera Virus
Well, I've done my best, but she needs to get shares in Polyfilla.

Phoebe

Do you mind, I am right here you know.

Mo

I've only got to look at my brandy bottle to know that.

Phoebe

Don't tell me, you three are teetotal.

Mo

Of course.

Phoebe

I'm the Queen of Sheba.

Mo/Carol/Vera Virus

Your Majesty. *(They curtsey)*

Phoebe

You will be saying you're virgins next.

Mo/Carol/Vera Virus

We are.

Phoebe

Virgin's on the ridiculous. *(They all laugh)*

Carol

Right, let's get you into your dress.

Mo

Phoebe you look beautiful. Go and look at yourself in the mirror.

As Phoebe looks into the mirror, a tear trickles down her cheek. They all stand next to her as they look in the mirror.

Carol

Now there's a princess.

The taxi driver beeps his horn.

Mo

Ladies, the taxi is here. *(After they all kiss Phoebe, Carol and Vera Virus get into the taxi)* Billy where are you?

Billy

I'm coming. *(He races down the stairs with a baseball cap on)* You look beautiful Aunty Phoebe. I hope I meet someone as beautiful as you when I get married.

Phoebe

Thank you, you super boy.

Mo

But you won't meet anyone as beautiful as your Aunty Phoebe wearing a baseball cap, take it off now.

Billy

Aunty Mo,

Mo

Now. *(Billy takes it off)* Now go and sulk in the taxi. *(Billy walks out the door)*

Ron comes down the stairs.

Ron

Miss Dickson you look wonderful.

Phoebe

Thank you kind sir.

Mo

Ron, let me take a look at you. You need to straighten your tie and give your shoes a polish. Right, I'm off. Your car will be here in twenty minutes and yes Phoebe, you have got time for another brandy. I'll see you in a bit and Ron don't forget to feed the cat. *(Mo rushes out and gets into the taxi)*

Twenty minutes later the taxi pulls up outside the church. Carol and Vera Virus get out of the taxi and are met by their husbands.

Carol

(To Tony) Look at the state of your shoes. It looks as though you have been gardening in them.

Tony

The taxi was late and I was standing there waiting, I noticed some weeds growing inbetween the flowers. Then there was some roses that needed dead-heading.

Carol

I don't want to hear any more. The only thing I'll be using is weed killer on you.

Vera Virus

(To Bert) Why are you wearing that suit?

Bert

You said I was to wear the suit that was hanging up in the bedroom.

Vera Virus

The one that was hanging up in the spare bedroom. The one that I had cleaned and pressed for you. Have you heard of hearing aids you deaf old fool. Why do we bother Carol.

Carol

Who knows Vera love, who knows. *(They walk into the church)*

Mo

(Walking up to the church) Billy, go and find me a place to sit. I want to talk to Ben. *(Billy runs into the church)*

Ben Hung

Hello Mrs Johnson.

Mo

Hello young man. You don't look to happy to say you are going to marry the lovely Phoebe in the next half a hour.

Ben Hung

I'm very happy, it's just that I must be the only groom without a best man.

Mo

Is that right? Well, if you look at the bottom of the path, I think you find those two young men will make the perfect best men.

With tears streaming down his cheeks, Ben gives Mo a huge hug and runs down the church path, picking up Gary and then hugging his brother, Simon.

Ben Hung

It's great to see you both. How did you know I was getting married?

Simon

You have a saint in this village, whose love and generosity knows no bounds.

Mo

Come on you three, the bride has just pulled up.

Ben Hung
(*Walking into the church*) Thank you.

Mo
You are very welcome.

Waving at Ron and Phoebe, Mo goes into the church and sits next to Billy at the front.

Frigging Freda
I see 'Pissed up Pete who likes it neat' is swaying.

Janice
It's like looking at the leaning tower of Pisa.

Harold
Carol, it's time to stand either side of Pissed up Pete who likes it neat.

Pissed up Pete
(*To Carol*) If you get any closer love my whole body will be in between your boobs.

Harold
You won't be the first vicar and certainly not the last. Many a man has found it is a heavenly place to be.

Carol
If only your man boobs had the same effect when it came to men. Hell springs to mind.

Harold
(*Whispering*) Bitch.

Carol
Slut.

Harold

Mo. *(Waving to him)*

Mo

He's slurring his words. You stand behind him and look over his shoulder. You whisper the wedding service a line at a time, so he can repeat your words.

Pissed up Pete

Well, I don't get this everyday. *(He starts to sing 'We are having a gang bang we are having a ball, we are having a gang bang against the wall'. Mo stamps on his foot)*

Phoebe and Ron walk down the aisle to the wedding march. Tommy and Jenny walk behind as the bridesmaid and page boy. As they get to the front Ron gives Phoebe's hand to Ben and the ceremony begins with Mo whispering the lines and Pissed up Pete repeating them. Gary gives Pissed up Pete the rings and, repeating after Mo, Pissed up Pete declares them husband and wife. They both walk up the aisle to the church's door where the photographer is waiting. After taking several pictures of the bride and groom, the next photo is taken with Simon and Gary on the groom's side and with Mo and Ron on the bride's side.

Photographer

Are there any more family members?

Phoebe

We are all family here.

Photographer

In that case, let's have everyone in please. That was brilliant. Thank you.

As he finishes, Pissed up Pete who likes it neat comes out of the church dancing. He is singing 'We are having a gang bang, we are having a ball'. When he gets to the steep bank, he loses his footing and falls down a newly dug grave.

Frigging Freda
With singing like that, he deserves an early grave. *(Everyone laughs)*

The bride and groom are seen driving away as everyone else walks down the hill towards the Queens Head.

Janice
Well I thought it was a lovely service.

Vera Virus
It was unique in our village.

Carol
You would have made a good vicar Mo.

Mini Meg
That's what the village family does best.

Frigging Freda
Don't you have to be pure and believe in the sanctity of marriage.

Harold
That's a non starter yet. *(Everyone nods their heads)*

Mo
Have you load of bitches finished? Get yourselves on your broomsticks and piss off *(Everyone laughs)*

Brenda
Well it's third time lucky.

Harold

That's the three we know about.

Mo

Right, that's it, come here you nasty queen. *(Mo chases Harold to the door of the Queen's Head)*

Harold

I think we are getting a bit old for all this chasing around.

Mo

I think my days of chasing men are well and truly over.

Harold

I came to that conclusion when I couldn't catch them up. The hottest thing that ever gets in my mouth these days is a cup of tea. *(They both laugh)* Right, come on girl lets get in, I've got the entertainment to sort out.

As they both walk in they both take a bucks fizz off the waiters tray. Mo walks up to Phoebe and Ben, who are waiting to greet their guests, and they hug each other at the same time.

Phoebe

(With a tear in her eye) If it wasn't for you, none of this would be happening.

Mo

The Lord always shines on the righteous.

Phoebe

Thank you.

As Mo goes off to find a place to sit all the other guests walk in. They all greet Phoebe and Ben in turn.

Harold

Thank you everyone, thank you. Shut your mouths. Now I have your attention, I would like to ask the best man to come on the stage to give his speech. Sexy Simon everyone. *(Everyone claps)*

Simon

Thank you everyone. Well, I must admit that I must be the least prepared best man ever, due to the fact that this is the first time I've seen my brother in nearly twenty years. Although I will say his love and generosity, knows no bounds. When we were growing up, if it wasn't for my wonderful brother, then it would be very doubtful whether I would be standing here today. So all I can say to my brother and his beautiful wife, is congratulations and I hope each day together will be a happy one. Please stand and raise your glasses, the bride and groom.

Everyone

The bride and groom.

Simon

It's now time to read out some of the cards. To Phoebe and Ben, congratulations to you both. Phoebe could you please return my iron you borrowed, two years ago, you robbing cow. Love from Dilys and Philys. The next card. Congratulations to you both, Phoebe if you ever split up, could you send Ben round to my place as I've got a lot of cobwebs that need cleaning down below. Love from Yvette.

Phoebe

She wants to try soap and water for a change. *(Everyone laughs)*

Simon

Let's try a couple more. Congratulations to you both. Phoebe could you please return my hairdryer as I'm sure your forest down below never gets wet enough at your age to be needing a hairdryer. Love from Harold *(Everyone laughs, Phoebe can be seen sticking two fingers up, as Harold blows her a kiss.)* Lets do one more. Phoebe, when are you going to pay for the four bottles of gin, two bottles of vodka and the bottle of brandy you had last month, you drunken tart. Congratulations to you both from the staff of the offie.

Harold
Thank you sexy Simon.

Simon
You're welcome Hot Harold. *(Harold goes bright red as everyone cheers and claps)*

Harold
Now the groom.

Ben Hung
Thank you Simon for that heartfelt speech. I'm so glad we both survived. I want to thank my beautiful wife for agreeing to marry me and for giving me a home, I love being in, especially as I now know every inch of it from the top to bottom. As well as the house it's great to be in the garden in all weathers on my hands and knees with just an apron on and my beautiful wife, under her umbrella, booting my bottom and telling me to pull the weeds out quicker.

Mo
What a kind thoughtful woman she is.

Phoebe
That's quality for you.

Ben Hung
Raise your glasses everyone. The bride.

Everyone
The bride.

Ben Hung

Now, I must say a few thank yous. To Meg, I would like to thank you and your cookery class for the wonderful food we have today. My wife and the good people of the village would like Penny to show off her fingers to everyone, so they can still see she is still wearing plasters on every finger. *(Penny stands up and shows her fingers, everyone cheers)* I would also like to thank Carol and Vera for making my wife look so beautiful.

Vera Virus

It took some doing. *(Everyone laughs)*

Ben Hung

I would also like to thank Brenda and Dick for lending us their children.

Dick

Any time. We will lend them to you next Saturday, as we need a babysitter. *(Everyone laughs)*

Ben Hung

Also a big thank you to Hot Harold, for getting us the Queens Head at such short notice. I'm sure my brother will thank you personally at the end of the night. *(Harold blushes and the crowd cheers)* But there is one amongst you that just brought so much love and kindness with her, that to call her a friend is an amazing honour. Thank you from both of our hearts. *(Mo gets up and walks onto the stage. She puts her arms around a tearful Ben as everyone claps)*

Mo

You, young man are too kind and as Phoebe will tell you, all family sticks together *(Everyone stands and cheers)* Now I know by now you all must be starving, but I would just like to give Phoebe and Ben my present. As you know, there was a five year old boy called Gary, who was one of Ben's best men, but for the last three hours he has not been seen. I know this because Ben has been looking and asking everyone, isn't that right Ben?

Ben Hung

It is Mrs Johnson.

Mo

Well, after the church service a super teacher by the name of M M took him back to his foster parents and collected all of his belongings and they went round to your place. Letting themselves in, they unpacked all of Gary's things in his new bedroom. Then he dashed back to be with his new Mum and Dad. Here are the legal documents that make him your son. Come on Gary, come and meet your new parents. *(Gary runs onto the stage an jumps into Ben's arms)*

Vera Virus

She thinks she is Cilla now.

Ben Hung

Thank you so much.

Mo

You are very welcome. Ladies and gentlemen, the buffet is now open. *(Everyone claps and cheers)*

After about a hour, Harold comes onto the stage to announce the bingo.

Harold

It's bingo time, make sure you all have your cards, as the prizes are amazing.

Vera Virus

If they are, does that mean Phoebe hasn't donated any of her out of date food?

Phoebe

I don't know what you mean. *(They all laugh)*

Mo

Phoebe, you and Ben come and sit next to me, I've got your cards.

Phoebe

Do I have to?

Mo

Yes you do. There are some fabulous prizes to be won.

Phoebe

But I never win on these things.

Mo

You have got to be in it to win it.

Harold

Right ladies and gentleman, we are playing for the four corners. Number 22, Phoebes kicked her husband with her shoe. Number 84, Phoebe's husband cleans the floor. Number 14, Phoebe's husband cleans the toilet seat.

Simon

Yes!

Harold

Come onto the stage *(Simon walks onto the stage and stands next to Harold)* Well let's see what you have won. A meal for two at Mr Wong's.

Simon

I wonder who I am going to take with me. *(Flirting with Harold)*

Harold

Whoever it is, I hope they are quality.

Simon

They certainly are.

Harold

Right everyone, it's now time for the middle line. Number 8, How did Mo miss her mouth again.

Mo

Sod off.

Harold

Number 28, Janice dreams of fitting into a size 8.

Janice

I'm only two sizes away.

Everyone

Specsavers.

Harold

Number 3, Tony is on bended knee pulling the weeds out three by three.

Ben Hung

Yes!

Harold

It seems we have a winner. Come up onto the stage and we will see what you have won. Well, this is strange, it's a picture. What is the picture Ben?

Ben Hung

It's a greenhouse.

Harold

Not only is it a picture of a greenhouse, but that greenhouse is being delivered to your house next weekend. *(Everyone claps)*

Ben Hung

I've never had a present as big as this before. Thank you everyone. *(Being close to tears, Ben gets off the stage and walks over to Mo, and gives her a big hug)*

Harold

Right everyone, eyes down for a full house. Number 99, Tony is putting washing on the line. Number 88, Tony is ironing Carol's smalls again. Number 6, Harold loves big feet. *(Everyone cheers)* Number 11, this village is heaven. *(Everyone stands up and claps)*

Phoebe

Bingo!

Harold

I think we have a winner. Come onto the stage young lady and lets see what you have won. *(Phoebe does this)*

Phoebe

I can't believe this, I never win anything.

Harold

Everything comes to those who wait, and by the looks of the prizes this was worth waiting for. Ben come and join us, On Monday morning you will both be getting the ten o'clock train to Southampton. From there, you will board the ship 'The Sea Princess' and spend the next ten nights cruising around the Mediterranean, visiting Rome and Venice, then onto Barcelona and stopping three nights in the south of France. *(A tearful Phoebe hugs both Ben and Harold)*

Phoebe

But wait a minute, we don't have passports?

Mo

(Standing up) You do now. *(Showing their passports)*

Phoebe

You are wonderful. But wait a minute, I'm a mother with a child.

Mo

And I know a wonderful mother who has a spare bed.

Phoebe

Believe me, that woman is wonderful. *(They both walk off the stage and group hug Mo)*

Harold

Right everyone, get your phones out. It's cake cutting time.

After cutting the cake, Mini Meg cuts the cake into pieces and Phoebe and Ben hand out the pieces to everyone.

Mo

Meg this cake tastes beautiful.

Mini Meg

Penny gave me a hand.

Mo

It just shows you what plasters on a girls fingers can achieve.

Harold

Ladies and gentlemen, it's time for the happy couple to take their first dance together. *(With Lionel Richie's 'Endless Love' playing, Ben and Phoebe take to the dance floor)*

Mo

The way she is moving, they will be applying to go on Come Dancing next year.

As they are dancing, Ben Hung accidentally treads on Phoebe foot.

Phoebe

(To Ben) You want to remember this is the foot that got you here today. *(As the music stops playing, Phoebe boots him up the bum)*

Ben

Sorry Mistress.

Mo

Maybe not.

Harold

It's time for the act you have all been waiting for. Just flown in from Las Vegas. *(The Fella Bella pops her head out of the stage door)*

The Fella Bella

We have just come back from Skeggy.

Harold

The wonderful, the amazing, Sonny and Cher.

Policeman Mickey is Char and the Fella Bella is Sonny. They both sing 'I've Got You Babe', followed by 'If I Could Tun Back Time' and 'Believe.' Everyone gets up and starts to dance.

Simon

(Sitting next to Ben) These people are amazing. They are so kind and generous.

Ben Hung

That's why, when you come to this village you never leave.

Simon

I would never want to. Where is Hot Harold? *(He goes off to look for him)*

Elevated

Characters

Mo, Ron, Michael, Billy, Carol and Tony, Brenda and Dick, Harold and Mary, Tommy and Jenny, Phoebe and Ben Hung, Gary and the Old Man.

Setting

Mo's cottage, the river

Elevated

Mo and Billy are talking in the kitchen.

Billy
Aunty Mo.

Mo
Yes Billy?

Billy
Why is it when it comes to the summer holidays the time goes so quickly?

Mo
You want to be grateful that for you it's just the summer holidays. For me it's the whole year.

Billy
That's the last thing you need at your age..

Mo
Do you want your legs slapping young man?

Billy
I thought that's what Wonder Woman Gill is for?

Mo
She does it very well. That's why there is a long waiting list to see her.

Billy
No offence Aunty Mo, but when it comes to slapping my legs I'll wait for a professional to do it.

Mo

Come here and give me a hug.

Billy

Aunty Mo. *(He walks over and gives Mo a big hug)*

Mo

Right, what are we going to do today? You're back at school next week.

Billy

I did think about going for a picnic, like we did last year, but Uncle Ron is very grumpy today.

Mo

Grumpy Uncle Ron got four numbers on the lottery, but forgot to get his ticket. Let's ask him. *(Mo shouts for Ron)* Grumpy Uncle Ron are you there?

Ron

(Coming in from the garden) Less of the grumpy young lady. What can I do for you two?

Mo

You know Billy's back at school next week, and the nights are drawing in, we thought about going for a picnic by the river.

Ron

What and have the world and his wife come and join us?

Mo

We can find a nice quiet spot where no-one will find us. Besides, its Bank Holiday Monday, they will all be off doing other things.

Ron

I'm not sure. *(He goes back into the garden)*

There is a knock at the door.

Billy
I'll go.

Michael
Hello you super boy. *(Bill jumps into Michael's arms and gives him a big hug. He carries Billy into the kitchen)*

Mo
Hello, what are you doing here? *(Putting Billy down, he hugs his mother)*

Michael
There was a client I had to see in the next village and as the meeting only took a hour, I thought I would spend the rest of the day with my beautiful mother.

Mo
It's wonderful to see you. Sit down, I'll put the kettle on.

Billy
Me and Aunty Mo was hoping to go for a picnic by the river to-day, but grumpy Uncle Ron doesn't want to go, because he got four numbers on the lottery but didn't get his ticket.

Michael
Shall I go and have a word with grumpy Uncle Ron?

Billy
That would be great if you could.

Michael
Leave it to me. *(He goes into the garden)*

Mo

Right, Billy go and get your football, but no phone and definitely no tennis rackets. It took your Aunty Carol a week to get rid of her chesty cough.

Billy

With her chest, I'm surprised it was only a week.

Mo

Less of your lip young man. Go.

Michael and Ron come in from the garden.

Michael

You will be glad to hear that grumpy Uncle Ron is grumpy no more.

Mo

What changed his mind?

Michael

I've given him a dead cert at the two-thirty at Haydock.

Mo

Get the car out Ron.

Michael

We can go in mine.

Mo

No we can't. You have been driving all morning.

Ron

But it's a forty grand BMW.

Mo

I couldn't care less. I want both my boys in the back, where I can keep an eye on them. Michael, you can take the food and Billy put your phone on the table now.

Billy

Aunty Mo.

Mo

Now!

Billy puts his phone on the table and they all walk out to the car.

Ron

Are we all in? Then off we go.

Mo

Michael, if you give my husband another dead cert, you will find yourself grounded, now that is a dead cert.

Michael

Sorry Mum.

Billy

Wow, so even though Michael is rich, married with his own children he can still be grounded. What chance have I got. *(They all laugh)*

After half a hour, they arrive at the river.

Ron

Where do you want to be?

Mo

There is some trees further up, we can be nice and private there.

Driving to the trees, they park the car and carry everything down the river.

Michael

Where do we want them?

Mo

Put the deck chairs over there and the food down here.

Ron

I've just forgotten something in the car. I will be back in a minute.

Mo

I bet you will. Billy, don't go near the water. You know what happened to Aunty Carol.

Michael

What did happen to Mrs Bloomer?

Mo

She fell in the river playing tennis with Phoebe. It gave her a chesty cough for a week.

Michael

Just a week? I would've thought it would have been longer.

Mo

That's what that young man said and he's only ten.

Michael

Well, she is noticeable to all ages. *(They both laugh)*

Ron comes back from the betting office.

Ron

(Sitting on a deck chair) Now this is the life, relaxing with my beautiful family.

Mo

If you have put any more than a tenner on, you will be relaxing in the spare bedroom tonight.

Five minutes later. Carol and Tony are walking down the bank, arguing.

Carol

(To Tony) Will you shut up about your bloody tomatoes.

Ron

Here we go. Those are the first.

Carol

Hello everyone. Tony put my deck chairs next to Mo.

Mo

Did I hear you were having words?

Carol

There will be more than words if he carries on.

Mo

What has he done?

Tony

You mean, what has she done.

Carol

Do you know Mo, I was watching Emmerdale when all of a sudden I thought I'll go into the garden and help my lovely husband. I went into the greenhouse and thought I would water the tomatoes as they looked a bit droopy. Unbeknownst to me, I pick up a watering can that he uses to wash his paint brushes with. Who uses a watering can to clean their paint brushes?

Mo
How's the tomatoes looking?

Carol
Like a bloke on a Saturday night who's had ten pints.

Mo
Not good.

Carol
No.

Tony
They were great tomatoes.

Carol
Shut up. At least you have something in common with them and you haven't had ten pints.

Billy
Hello Aunty Carol.

Carol
Hello you beautiful boy. I say Mo, did that beautiful son of yours, come out your vagina?

Mo
He did Carol.

Michael
Hello Mrs Bloomer.

Carol
Hello you beautiful man. *(She winks at him)*

Ten minutes later, to the music of Titanic, Ben Hung is holding Phoebe up. She has her arms stretched out wide. Gary is walking behind, carrying the deck chairs, the food and the drink.

Ron
Round two.

Phoebe
Hello everyone. I was just reconstructing our wonderful cruise.

Putting her down, Phoebe goes round kissing everyone.

Ben Hung
Where would you like your chair?

Phoebe
Next to Mo would be good. *(Sitting down)* I say Mo.

Mo
Yes Phoebe?

Phoebe
Did that handsome man really come out of your vagina?

Mo
Yes Phoebe love, every inch of him.

Phoebe
There certainly looks to be a lot of inches.

Michael
Hello Mrs Clarkson.

Phoebe

Hello Michael. Are you having trouble at home?

Michael

No, everything is fine.

Phoebe

Well, you remember, there is always a bed at my place. Especially now we have Gary. There are times Ben needs a bit of help around the house.

Mo

You are so thoughtful.

Phoebe

Well I don't know about you lot but I am in need of a glass of something.

Carol

That would go down just nicely.

Phoebe

Gary, get the glasses out and bring Aunty Phoebe a bottle of wine.

Mo

Not mummy then?

Phoebe

I just feel too young to be called Mummy. His father is much more hands on with him. I'm lucky if I see him twice a day. *(Gary gives Phoebe the glasses and then the bottle of wine)* You are a good boy. Tony, Ron, Michael, do you fancy a beer?

Ron

That's kind of you.

Phoebe

Gary get three tins out of the cooler. *(Gary does this and gives them to Tony, Ron and Michael)* Cheers everyone.

Everyone

Cheers.

Harold and Mary comes down the bank.

Mo

Harold, before you ask did Michael come out of my vagina, he did.

Harold

I bet it makes a change for something to come out instead of going in. It always did see lot of daylight. *(Everyone laughs)*

Mary

Hello Aunty Mo.

Mo

Hello you beautiful girl. The first year out of the way.

Mary

It's gone so quick, can I talk to you later?

Mo

Of course you can.

Harold

I could just do with a glass.

Phoebe

Gary, fetch me another glass.

Carol

Here comes the birthday boy.

Mo

Hello Brenda.

Brenda

Hello Mo. Hello everyone. *(She kisses everyone)* Tommy what do you say to Aunty Mo?

Tommy

Thank you Aunty Mo for my money.

Mo

Come and give me a hug.

Brenda

What do you say to Aunty Phoebe?

Tommy

Thank you Aunty Phoebe for the tins of fruit. Especially as they were only one day out of date this year. *(They all look at Phoebe)*

Phoebe

You are very welcome flower.

Brenda

Aunty Carol.

Tommy

Thank you Aunty Carol for my seeds. The tomatoes seeds you gave me last year are doing great. I have got some wonderful big juicy tomatoes.

Tony

Mine was the same up until yesterday. They are all dead now.

Carol

Shut up. Carry on and you will go the same way.

Phoebe

Wine Brenda? Dick, a beer?

Brenda

That would be nice.

Phoebe

Gary get me another glass and you better bring me another bottle and a beer for Uncle Dick.

Harold

Here you are young man. *(He gives Tommy a card)*

Tommy

(Opening the card) Thank you Uncle Harold.

Brenda

You are a lucky boy. You better give it to me to save.

Carol

Twenty pounds. You didn't spend much the other night then?

Harold

I had a very nice evening. I didn't spend a thing. I would also like you to know I didn't look at the waiters once. Even when they bent down to pick things up.

Phoebe

It must be love. Did you take him back to your's for dessert?

Harold

How dare you. I'm not that type of girl.

Phoebe

Of course you aren't.

Mo

Are you seeing him again?

Harold

He is staying with me next weekend. Before you ask, he will be in the spare room. *(Everyone bursts out laughing)* You vile witches.

Carol

Harold, once a slut always a slut.

Ron

Shall we go and have a game of football?

Ben Hung

That sounds good Mr Johnson.

Carol

Ron take Tony, his miserable face is putting me off my wine.

All the men go off to play football. As they walk over, Ron tells them about the two-thirty at Haydock.

Ron

You have got half an hour before the race.

Ben Hung

I've got the app, we can do it now. *(Getting the app up)* It's a hundred to one outsider.

Ron

Normally I wouldn't go anywhere near it, but if Michael is giving you a tip, you take it. Twenty pounds gets you a thousand.

Tony

A bit rich for me.

Ben Hung

I don't think I will bother Mr Johnson.

Dick

Brenda will kill me if she finds out I've been betting.

Ron

You have been warned.

Mo

Brenda, is it me or is there something bothering you?

Brenda

(Bursting out into tears) I'm pregnant.

Carol

That's wonderful news. Isn't it?

Brenda

The scan showed there was a fifty percent chance that the baby could be disabled in some way.

Mo

That's a fifty percent chance, not a hundred.

Phoebe

What has Dick said?

Brenda

Not much really. He's of the mind that why chance it when we already have two healthy children.

Phoebe

Typical bloke. Always settle for what they have got, never takes a chance for more.

Mo

What do you want to do?

Brenda

I want to have it.

Mo

Then have it.

Brenda

But what if the child is severely handicapped? Yes I can cope with its needs, but then one day, I will not be here and it will be left to the child's brother and sister to look after them. It's not fair on them.

Mo

But Brenda, you are looking at the worst scenario. Who's to say the child will have any handicap.

Carol

I had three miscarriages, that left me to never be a mother. I had to watch my friends and family bring up their own children, receiving so much and contentment while they were doing it. So even if it had just been a fifty percent chance, I would have taken it in a heartbeat. It tortured me for years, before I could come to terms with it. Don't put yourself in hell for what could be the rest of your life.

Brenda

I have got a few weeks left to decide.

Mo
> You know where we are, day and night.

Brenda
> Thank you.

All of a sudden, there is loud shouting and cheering coming from the playing field.

Harold
> Is that Ron?

Phoebe
> He must of scored a goal.

Mo
> He's scored a goal alright, but I think its of horsey nature. Come on Mary, lets go and tell them the food is ready.

Mary
> *(Walking up to the playing field)* Do you think Brenda will have the child

Mo
> I don't think, I know she will. You see Mary, the female body is designed for the purpose of having children. There are those women who choose not to have children, but women like Brenda, who for so long thought they could never have children, cannot fight against what their body was designed for. Brenda was born to be a mother.

Mary
> But what if the child is disabled in some way?

Mo
> Even if there is a chance the baby might be disabled, the mater-

nal force of having her own baby is just too strong for Brenda. Dick can say and threaten what he likes, but the baby growing inside her will win every time. Now, what is it you want to talk to me about?

Mary

Thinking ahead Aunty Mo, when I get to the end of my degree, I would like to do an MA in finance, which will mean me studying for an extra year.

Mo

Mary, the reason I chose your Uncle Harry to adopt you was because I knew a bright girl like you would want to go to university and beyond. Now you know and I know, it's not cheap to do these things. To have the debt around your neck day in and day out, can make life unbearable. Believe me, I've been to hell and back. But your Uncle Harold is a wealthy man and giving him a child that he loves and adores, the money side of things you don't need to worry about. All I and your mother want is for you to work hard and achieve your goals. Now, give me a big hug. *(Mary does this)*

Mary

Thank you Aunty Mo. Sometimes I find myself looking up to the sky at night and looking at the stars.

Mo

Is there a star that shines the brightest?

Mary

There is.

Mo

That's your mother's star, shining her love to you. She always said she would be with you every minute of the day. Make us proud Mary.

Mary

I will.

Mo

Ron Johnson, what is making you run and shout like a lunatic?

Ron

It romped in at one hundred to one.

Carol

Ron, what are you so happy about?

Ron

I just won a thousand pounds at the two-thirty at Haydock.

Carol

Congratulations. It' a shame you didn't share your knowledge.

Ron

I did, but they were not interested. Your Tony said it was too rich for him.

Carol

My fool of a husband strikes again. Too rich? That's one thing he will never be.

Brenda

Ron where do you get your tip from?

Ron

Michael gave it to me.

Brenda

So a millionaire, who is in the know, gives you a tip and you don't bother?

Dick

What would you say to me having a bet?

Brenda

Nothing, because you would've won.

Dick

You moan if I do, you moan if I don't.

Mo

Lets move on.

Phoebe

We can when Ben tells us why he didn't have a bet.

Ben Hung

I thought you would be cross?

Phoebe

You're right, I am cross. When you get a tip from a beautiful man in the know...

Mo

(To Ron) Happy now are we?

Ron

Don't have a go at me. I told them to put a bet on.

Mo

Well I'm now telling you to drop it.

Harold

I wasn't ever asked.

Mo

I'm asking you to drop it.

Phoebe

Let's face it Carol, you always did lose out.

Carol

What's that supposed to mean?

Phoebe

Look at last year when you lost to me at tennis.

Carol

I tripped.

Phoebe

Of course you did.

Carol

There are two rowing boats over there. I'll race you to the other side and back.

Phoebe

You're on.

Mo

Come on ladies, lets think about this.

Carol

I've thought how I'm going to wipe that smile off her smug face.

Phoebe

We will see about that.

They both walk down to the river and get into the boats.

Carol

(To Phoebe) Three oars in a boat.

Phoebe

Piss off you big tits tart. Billy you can start us off.

Billy

Aunt Mo.

Mo

You can thank Uncle big mouth Ron for this.

Billy

(Walking down to the river) On your marks, get set, go.

Both women make a dash for it, splashing at each other as they go. With everyone at the side of the river cheering, an old man comes over to speak to Mo.

Old Man

Excuse me love, but what are those two idiots doing?

Mo

Trying to prove a point.

Old Man

The point is love, both of these boats have got holes in. I was going to use them for fire wood. Whose going to compensate.

Mo

You leave that to me. Five hundred sort it?

Old Man

That would do very nicely.

Mo

I'll send my husband round in the morning.

As they both reach the other side together, they turn their boats around and start their journeys back. As they get to the middle of the river, both ladies can be heard shouting that their boats are sinking . About three metres from the shore, the boats both sink and both Phoebe and Carol are left floating in the water, screaming. Ron, Dick and Ben run into the water to save them. Five minutes later, they are all walking out of the water dripping.

Carol

(To Tony) I see you didn't bother to save me.

Tony

You could say that about my tomatoes.

Mo

I hope the water has cooled you all down a bit. Now you can see Ron, why we don't talk about money in public. Money will never come between our extended family.

Billy

Why are the churches ringing their bells?

Mo

(Collapsing to her knees in floods of tears) I have waited for this moment for many years.

Michael comes over to his mother and picks her up.

Michael

Are you alright?

Mo

I am now Your Grace. *(She curtseys)*

Michael

What do you mean?

Mo

You are the next in line to the Dukedom.

Michael

Don't be silly, I can't be a Duke.

Mo

You can and you are.

Michael starts to cry on his mother's shoulder. People start to appear on the bank. Phoebe comes up to Michael and curtseys. She is followed by everyone else with the women curtseying and the men bowing.

Michael

Thank you everyone.

Mo

Ron you need to take His Grace to the manor.

Ron

But I'm soaking wet.

Mo

Ron, just do it please.

As Michael and Ron go up the bank to the car, people are calling out 'Your Grace' and bowing.

Phoebe

Do you want a lift?

Mo

That would be good of you.

Phoebe

Well we can't have the Dowager Duchess walking home can we?

The First Of December

Characters

Mo, Phoebe, Carol, Vera Virus, Harold, Janice, Bucket Bill, Ron, Ben Hung, Burt Tony, Gary and Sweaty Betty.

Setting

The Museum's Dungeon, the Christmas market.

The First Of December

The committee members are sitting around a table in the dungeon.

Harold

Good afternoon ladies and welcome to our half-yearly committee meeting. Now before we start, a certain individual a few months ago found herself elevated to new heights, as she became the Dowager Duchess. This allows her to be addressed as 'Her Grace' so how would you like to be addressed by us today?

Mo

To my nearest and dearest, just address me as you always have done.

Phoebe

Slut.

Carol

Tart.

Vera Virus

Bitch.

Harold

Witch. I'm so glad we cleared that up. Mrs Johnson as the treasury secretary, could you make your report.

Mo

Thank you Mr Chairman and my fellow bitches. In the last six months, we have financially seen our profits go through the roof. As you can see in your booklets, the bus company last year has made fifty-thousand in the first year, and the surplus has doubled. Like the bus company, slave membership has doubled in size within a six month waiting list. This has seen the surplus double in the first six months. Six months ago I calculated the gas, electric and water on last year's figures. However, with the managing directors of both gas and electric now slave members, these bills have halved. Also, getting the permission from the chairman, to move the director of water from the waiting list, to a full time member, we have now seen our water bills halved as well. We have also allowed the bank manager quick access to full member status. Our business accounts now get a ten percent interest gain on our accounts.

Phoebe

Talk about not what you know, but who you know.

Mo

As a committee member, you will see financial benefits, when you make an appointment to see the bank manager. When you do go and see him, make sure you wear something revealing and short. While at it the meeting, make sure you drop something and when you are picking it up, do it in full view of the bank manager. With your expertise in this field you should all come out of the bank millionaires. In your case, remember your transsexual days. One last point, with our finances looking so good, I propose that all members of staff get a Christmas bonus.

Harold

On giving the staff a Christmas bonus, please raise your hands. *(Everyone raises theirs)* That is carried.

Mo

Finally, for everyone's hard work in the last six months, I have an envelope for you. *(She passes the envelopes around)*

Phoebe

Two thousand pounds. You are wonderful. *(They all get up and give Mo a hug)*

Harold

Thank you Mrs Johnson. We now go over to our public relations executive.

Vera Virus

Thank you Mr Chairman. Well if I say so now myself, our advertising campaign has gone very well. All the businesses that have displayed our posters have reported their profits up. There was talk that Mrs Bloomer could be the new face of the five pound note. Although they would have to make the note bigger which would increase the five pound notes, to seven pounds fifty. This would make each breast one pound twenty-five pence each. However the Bank of England just can't get a breast of the idea, as of yet. With our posters doing so well I thought we would move into the t-shirt advertising as well Mrs Clarkson would you like to model it for us? *(Phoebe removes her coat of reveal a t-shirt with a young man on all fours, having his naked bottom kicked. Phoebe is walking up and down the dungeon, showing it off)* I would like to take this opportunity to thank Mrs Clarkson, as it is her foot that is kicking her husband's bottom.

Harold

I'll have two.

Vera Virus

The slogan 'A man is not just for Christmas, he is for life,' is telling the people that these t-shirts and the museum are not here for a short time, but for life. We have acquired, a stall at the Christmas Market tonight, so I hope everyone gives a hand.

Harold

Thank you, Mrs Winterbottom. Before I move on to Mrs Bloomer's special announcement, I would just like to say the reason you can see a slave hanging whilst cleaning the chandelier is because he likes to get his money's worth. Mrs Bloomer, your announcement.

Carol

Thank you Mr Chairman. As you know, I have been showing the visitors around the museum for the last six months, something I have thoroughly enjoyed. But due to personal issues at home, I will need to go down to part time after Christmas.

Mo

Everything alright love?

Carol

It's that husband of mine. Things are starting to slide at home. Yesterday when I got home, I found him sitting in my chair marking off the programmes he was going to watch. Now, that is bad enough, but I found he had marked off Naked Attraction and First Dates. It has rocked me to the core, especially as the times they are on he should be doing the downstairs dusting. *(Carol begins to cry)*

Mo

(Putting her arm around her) Carol we fully understand your dilemma. No-one wants to see their husband taking advantage, by not doing his jobs around the house. Part time will be fine.

Carol

Thank you Mo. It's a comfort to know that I won't be putting my finger into any dust.

Harold

Thank you Mrs Bloomer. We can only hope and pray that you get your home dust free very soon. Mrs Clarkson, can we have your report please.

Phoebe

Thank you Mr Chairman. As you know our recruitment of Miss Wonders, Mini Meg and Miss Bloomer has shown itself to be a great success. With Miss Wonders talents being talked about far and wide. Before I address the part time vacancy left by Mrs Bloomer, Mrs Bloomer I sympathise with your situations as I have always made it a priority that my husband's daily routine is to tackle the dust. Thank goodness he is keeping on top of it.

Vera Virus
And you as well.

Phoebe
I do have my needs Miss Winterbottom. As a full time worker and mother, I have very few pleasures in life.

Mo
I heard your husband had to draw you a map so you could find your way to work. And for being a mother, the last time you went to pick your son up, the teachers wouldn't let you as they had never seen you before. Even Gary wasn't sure who you were.

Phoebe
You nasty witch.

Mo
You lazy tart.

Harold
(Banging his gavel on the table) Can I have some order here. Carry on and you will both find yourselves on the naughty step again. Please continue Mrs Clarkson.

Phoebe
Thank you Mr Chairman. As you know for the last two weeks, Penny has had a very bad cold, which has sent shock waves around the museum. I know Mini Meg did put a large muzzle on Penny's face, which did cover both her mouth and nose, but unfortunately it didn't stop a cascade flowing every time Penny sneezed. So before Health and Safety come knocking on our door we had to send

her home. However luckily for us Mrs Freerange, the farmer's wife, was able to stand in due to the fact that he has had his chopper stolen. They found that using a rake didn't give it that same sexual atmosphere. So that we are not put in that position again, I propose Mrs Freerange be taken on for two days a week after Christmas.

Harold
Hands up all who agree? *(Everyone's hands goes up)* That's agreed.

Phoebe
Getting back to the position of part time tour guide, working alongside the amazing Mrs Bloomer was not easy to fill, but I have found an international superstar. So super that she has been seen on the front covers on magazines like Mayfair, Playboy and even Nuts.

Mo
Who?

Phoebe
The fabulous Stella.

Carol
No.

Vera Virus
I can't believe it.

Mo
Don't tell me she wants thousands of pounds an hour.

Phoebe
What she wants is to get into the world of dominatrices. Now with the slave membership increasing. I thought it would be good, if Mistress Wonders trains her up, then we can put the slaves on

either the afternoon or evening shifts.

Vera Virus
What will the Mistress name be?

Phoebe
Mistress Artois.

Mo
That sounds very French.

Phoebe
She thinks the French make better lovers. She said she was making love in Paris when all of a sudden two other French guys joined in and because they spoke so romantically she was happy to be in a foursome.

Harold
Lucky bitch. Can we vote on Phoebe's proposal. *(Everyone puts their hands up)* That's carried. Thank you Mrs Clarkson. Is there any more business? No? Meeting adjourned.

Vera Virus
Don't forget the Christmas market tonight.

With the usual kisses and hugs, everyone leaves the museum. A few hours later Mo arrives at the Christmas market where she finds Janice and Carol outside the council house.

Mo
Hello you two. *(They hug)*

Janice
How are you, Your Grace?

Mo

Janice, as a nearest and dearest, please call me Mo. It's so refreshing at times to hear your own name. Even when I go into the butchers, Perry Pete is addressing me as Your Grace this, Your Grace that. I went in the last week and he said 'would you like a bit of rump Your Grace.'

Carol

Not what you want to hear.

Mo

You're right its not, especially when he is saying, he would love to handle a pair of royal knickers on a piece of rump.

Janice

You don't need it.

Mo

You don't when there is a shop full of customers. So are you two waiting for the Mayor to switch on the lights?

Carol

He could light me up any time.

Janice

I know we are not sure which way he swings, but with his looks, he could swing it front or back and I would be happy.

Carol

I would love him to get lost in my boobs for days.

Mo

The size of your boobs, that would be a great possibility. *(They all laugh)*

Carol

Here he comes.

The Mayor

Your Grace, ladies and gentlemen, thank you for coming to our annual Christmas market and without further ado, I pronounce Christmas has begun. *(He pressed the button and the Christmas lights are switched on. Everyone cheers and claps)*

Janice

He is always a man of few words.

Carol

There is no need for a lot of talking in the bedroom.

Janice

The lights look far better this year.

Mo

They would do. Light bulb Larry has lost the contract, he was sent down for two years.

Carol

How did that happen?

Mo

He saved his best lights for the production of cannabis growing.

Carol

I smoked a joint once.

Mo

Just the once?

Carol

It made me hallucinate that my Tony was a royal prince who

had come to take me away to his castle.

Mo

That sounds nice.

Carol

It would have been, but I found myself waking up in the shed with a duster and a tin of polish covering my bits.

Mo

Where was the prince?

Carol

Watching Gardener's World! Never again.

The three of them stand next to Bucket Bill's stall.

Bucket Bill

Good evening Your Ladyship.

Mo

Good evening Bill.

Bucket Bill

What would you like?

Mo

I would like a ten year old boy called Billy to remember he has got another hour before he goes home to bed, school is in the morning.

Billy

Aunty Mo.

Bucket Bill

I've made you up a nice hamper, Your Ladyship.

Mo

That's very kind of you Bill. Billy can bring it in with him, in the next hour.

Billy

Aunty Mo.

Mo

I'll see you in a hour. *(They walk away from Bucket Bill's stall)*
Carol

He doesn't look well.

Mo

Lung cancer.

Carol

That's a shame.

Mo

He came to see me last week.

Carol

Is there nothing they can do?

Mo

It has spread to half of his body. But I will give Bill his due, he doesn't blame anyone but himself. As he said, the drinks, the fags and the poor diet over many years were always going to catch up with him in the end.

Carol

Has he got long?

Mo

He is hoping he will see Christmas out.

Carol

Your Billy will miss his weekends on the stall.

Mo

It's time he started to learn how to grow what he has been selling for the last two years. With a son who is a Duke with a large estate, it's time for the head gardener to learn and understand how the grounds of a large estate is maintained.

Carol

You know exactly what Billy's future will entail.

Mo

I have for sometime. I have always believe that families should stick together.

Janice

What is going on over there?

Carol

What is Phoebe doing?

Mo

That's one way of selling t-shirts.

As they walk to the t-shirt stall, they can see that Phoebe and Ben Hung are recreating the front of the t-shirt. Ben Hung is on all fours showing his naked bottom, and Phoebe is wearing stockings and stilettos. She has got her foot next to Ben Hung's bottom.

Carol

I'll give her her due, if something needs selling, she sells it.

Vera Virus

(Who is behind the stall) Do you know girls, since Phoebe has put her foot in it, the t-shirts have been selling like hot cakes.

Mo

A modelling career begins.

Vera Virus

Another ten minutes and we will be sold out.

Carol

Let's hope they can hold that pose for another ten minutes. Ben's bottom is starting to look a bit blue with the cold.

Mo

You could use it as a wine cooler. *(They all laugh)* I just fancy a doughnut, anyone want one?

Phoebe

Yes please, I need something hot inside me.

Mo

With this cold weather it won't be your husband. *(Mo gets two lots of doughnuts)* Come on girls, help yourself.

Janice

I shouldn't really, but it is Christmas.

Phoebe

Trouble is though Janice, Christmas is everyday for you.

Janice

Bitch.

Carol

I've dropped it down my frontage.

Mo

You won't find that any time soon, you better have another one.

Phoebe

(Brushing sugar off Mo's coat) I don't know how you missed your mouth? It can usually take a bus.

Mo

Just because you won't be riding on the number sixty-nine bus later, don't take your frustrations out on me. *(They all laugh)*

They all walk over to listen to the choir sing.

Sweaty Betty

Hello Your Grace.

Mo

Hello Betty, is it on or off?

Sweaty Betty

It's on Your Grace. I've developed a foot fetish. So when I'm in bed, it guides the men to my feet. It's like a light to a moth.

Mo

What have you decorated it with this year?

Sweaty Betty

Santas Your Grace.

Mo

That's nice.

Sweaty Betty

I'm hoping for a ride on Santa's sleigh.

Mo

It's about the only place she hasn't had a ride.

Carol

Will she ever go on the straight and narrow?

Mo

Not while she is bisexual. When she wants women she goes inside, when she wants men she stays on the outside.

Carol

So the best of both worlds then.

Janice

Where is Harold tonight?

Phoebe

Well, I've heard this Sexy Simon thing has moved to another level. So Harold is determined to get fit and lose some weight.

Mo

How's he doing that?

Phoebe

He's brought all the gear, leggings, arm bands, even a headband.

Mo

Has he joined a gym?

Phoebe

No. But he bought the Jane Fonda workout video. He has been watching it for two days sitting on his sofa, eating fish and chips.

Mo

No running then?

Phoebe

Just to the chippy.

As the choir sings Silent Night, Ron, Rony, Bert and Ben Hung creep up behind their wives and stand behind them with their arms around them. Billy and Gary stand in the front, as they all sing Silent Night.

Mo
You have all been to the pub haven't you?

Ron/Tony/Bert
We don't know what you mean. *(Everyone bursts out laughing)*

New Life This Christmas

Characters

Mo, Phoebe, Carol, Vera Virus, Harold, Mini Meg, Dick, Dilys and Philys.

Setting

The hairdressers.

New Life This Christmas

Mo walks into the hairdressers and is confronted by a salon that is full of Christmas decorations. Standing at the door is a large mechanical Santa that opens his coat to reveal breasts and a penis. It says 'Ho ho ho, have I got a shock for you limp dick.'

Mo

You have exceeded yourself this year Vera.

Vera Virus

You know our Bella, she just loves Christmas.

Mo

Although looking at your transsexual Santa, Santa is catering for everyone's needs this year. Hello Girls.

Phoebe/Carol

Hello Mo.

Mo

Thank you for your cards ladies. Do you think Phoebe love, putting a picture of you kicking Ben's bare bottom on a Christmas card is appropriate? Especially as you have put a white beard and a Santa hat on his bottom.

Phoebe

I'm glad you liked it. I had to give him a back, crack and sack wax before I put that beard on him. Although the waxing left him all red, it made it look like Santa's rosy cheeks.

Mo

What are you all doing this Christmas day?

Carol

There will be just the two of us this year. That husband of mine likes us to eat his home grown veg for Christmas dinner. He likes to pick out the carrots that look as though they have grown legs. He said they always reminded him of my legs.

Phoebe

That's nice.

Carol

The legs on the carrots last year were fat and knobbly. I threw them at him and said 'legs eleven Tony's jobs have gone up by 7.'

Mo

What about you Phoebe?

Phoebe

Well, now we have Gary it will just be the three of us. I can't expect my Ben to cook for thousands. I am giving him the afternoon off on Christmas day. Gary needs someone to open his presents with.

Mo

You are so kind.

Phoebe

Gary's needs in the afternoon, my needs in the evening. What more could a girl ask for?

Mo

What about you Vera?

Vera Virus

It will be a Christmas on the sofa. He feeds me sugared almonds in the hope that he can replace Santa's empty sack. But a couple of large whiskeys and he only gets to dream about it.

Mo

It looks like you have all got Christmas wrapped up. But if you change your minds let me know. *(Mo hands invitation cards to spend Christmas at the Manor)*

Carol

Mo that is so kind of you.

Mo

But I don't want to deprive you of Tony's veg.

Carol

He can stick his veg where the sun don't shine. We will be there.

Phoebe

With Ben's job rota it is difficult. But if he does overtime before we go I think we'll just manage it. Of course you will want your nearest and dearest by your side. We will be there to support you.

Vera Virus

With the drinks flowing all weekend, he will be so intoxicated that he won't touch me once. Of course we will come.

Mo

That didn't take much persuasion. I can see with the knitting you have got Philys and Dilys under the dryers.

Vera Virus

They always treat themselves to a cut and set at Christmas. They pay for each others.

Mo

Really?

Vera Virus

Don't ask. They used to treat themselves to a trip to the cinema.

But this one particular time, Dilys had to go to the toilet. So Philys said 'I'll go in and save you a seat.' Ten minutes later Dilys came out of the toilets and went into the wrong room. They had booked to see 'Sandra Saves the Day' but Dilys went into the one that was showing 'Santa Stores His Sack.'

Mo

Porn?

Vera Virus

Just a bit. Especially as Santa was still delivering his presents on New Year's Day. Looking for Philys, an old man in a raincoat told her to sit down, as she was putting them off their strokes. She sat next to a young man in a Santa hat who kept smiling at her, and being polite she smiled back. She gets her glasses out, but drops them on the floor. As she goes down to pick them up, her back gives way, leaving her mouth open in pain. The young chap saw this as his cue. Dilys forgot about her pain for the next ten minutes. She found out what presents Santa was sharing. As she said afterwards 'sharing is caring.' After that experience, she always carries a pack of three in her handbag.

Mo

No Bella today?

Vera Virus

No. She has gone shopping with Policeman Mickey. Bella wants to recreate her bedroom as a winter wonderland. She likes to wonder which Disney character will walk through her door.

Mo

Lets hope it is not Goofy.

Vera Virus

She is hoping for Pluto. She finds being on all fours so comforting.

Mo

Does she know which part of the world she is getting married in?

Vera Virus

Last time I heard it was going to be the Caribbean.

Mo

Is that because of the clear blue waters, the golden beaches or even the total relaxation?

Vera Virus

None of them.

Mo

Why the Caribbean then?

Vera Virus

Because Policeman Mickey wants to lick fruits he hadn't tried before.

Phoebe

All he needs is a tin opener. It would save them a lot of money.

Carol

(Looking through the window) I can't see Sweaty Betty with the choir?

Mo

You won't dear. She went inside last week. She fancied a bit of beast in her mouth this year.

Carol

She was out last year.

Mo

That's because she fancied a bit of leg, a middle leg. *(They laugh)*
Harold comes through the door.

Harold

Morning everyone.

Mo

Morning love.

Vera Virus

What brought you here today?

Harold

I've just popped in to see what Mo's doing this Christmas.

Mo

This is for you.

Harold

(Opening his invitation) That would be very nice. Thank you
my darling.

Mo

As you can see I've put plus two. How is it going?

Harold

Mo, I don't know what to do.

Mo

Come and sit down. I'm sure me and Aunty Carol will sort it out
for you. Don't worry about the sister in law, she can't hear a thing
under that dryer.

Harold

I'm frightened Mo, that I'm going to get hurt. I just keep thinking why does a beautiful young man, that is half my age, want to be with a guy like me. He must only want me for my money.

Carol

Let's think about this. You are a single guy with a great personality. You are kind, funny and very genuine. So why shouldn't you attract a guy of that age?

Mo

Everything is alright in the bedroom department?

Harold

Everything is great in the bedroom. Although I must admit, I can't get into as many positions as I once did. There is only so far my legs can open these days.

Carol

Tell me about it. The last time my legs opened they locked. I was walking like John Wayne for days.

Mo

He has reached his thirties, so he is mature enough to know what he wants. I know he hasn't got a drink or drug problem.

Harold

He would rather drink tea.

Mo

There you go.

Carol

I think you are letting the age difference dictate to you.

Mo

With his past life, I think he just wants a man that can show him love. Something I don't think he has experienced before.

Carol

If it's the money side of things that is bothering you, tell him that he must find a job and only do things that you can both afford.

Harold

How do I know that he will stay with me?

Mo

You don't, just like we don't know if our husbands will stay with us. Although in Carol's case, if her Tony said he was leaving he would be in a wooden box.

Carol

Too right.

Mo

Give yourself a six month trial. If it's not working after that time, then separate. It's better to have loved and lost then to never have loved at all.

Harold

(Hugging them both) Thank you. I've got to go to do a bit of shopping. I'll see you all later. *(Harold leaves the hairdressers)*

Mo

We should go and work for the Samaritans, we would save hundreds.

Carol

That wouldn't be a bad idea.

Mo

Really?

Carol

I'll look into it after Christmas.

Brenda comes into the hairdressers.

Carol

Here she comes, mother to be again.

Vera Virus

Are you sure you are just having the one?

Brenda

I hope so. I couldn't manage any more.

Mo

Get yourself sat down.

Brenda

(Sitting down) It's the last time I play postman's knock.

Mo

Next time return to sender, address unknown. *(They all laugh)*

Vera Virus

Just had a text off Freda. She has arrived safely.

Phoebe

Is it Norway she has gone?

Vera Virus

Yes. To visit her sister.

Phoebe

At least she will get some of the white stuff this year.

Vera Virus

To be honest, she gets it most Christmas'

Phoebe

She still seeing the plumber then?

Vera Virus

She is. He has unblocked her for years. Although when he is telling his wife at four in the morning that he was late because he had to unblock a woman's sinks around the front and back, she is skating on very thin ice. Another text from Freda. It says, "I have joined the mile high club. The pilot took me to a height of forty thousand feet and my ears popped on the way down."

Mo

We are going to have to have a word with that young lady. She is getting out of control.

Vera Virus

She has just text that she was fully in control of the plane for more than an hour.

Brenda

(*Shouting*) Mo!

Mo

What is it?

Brenda

My waters have just broken.

Mo

Right, let's get you out of this chair. Girls, drag that table over. *(They do this)* Now gently ladies, lift her onto it. *(With lots of screaming, Brenda lays down on the table)* Vera phone for the ambulance. Carol shout for Meg to get over here. Phoebe, phone Dick and tell him what's happening.

Carol

(*Shouting*) Meg get over here now. *(In the middle of 'Silent Night' Meg runs over the square and into the hairdressers)*

Vera Virus

I've phoned for an ambulance.

Mini Meg

I don't think she is going to hang on that long. Vera we need some water and some towels.

Vera Virus

I'm on it.

Phoebe

Dick is going frantic. He is on his way.

Mini Meg

Phoebe get her knickers off and pull up her dress.

Phoebe

I can see you brought these knickers from the market. I hope you went to Nicola Knickers stall. She has got a sale on. Two for a fiver.

Mo

Not now Phoebe love.

Mini Meg

Just keep taking deep breaths Brenda. To be honest, the size you are, I will be surprised if there is only one baby inside of you.

Brenda

(Fighting the pain) That's all that showed up on the scan.

Mini Meg
But babies can stack up behind each other.

Dilys and Philys notice what it going on and get up out of their seats with their knitting.

Philys
Well would you believe it Dilys, it's happening again.

Dilys
Come on girl, lets have a closer look. *(They walk over to the table that Brenda is lying on)*

Philys
Dilys, don't bother feeling her legs, you will get your nails caught up. In fact, she has got more hair on these legs than next door's dog.

Dilys
Has she ever heard of waxing?

Philys
Obviously not. Mind you with her love life, she is never going to burn the candle at both ends, so why wax.

They both sit down at the opposite end of the table, doing their knitting.

Dilys
(Looking at Brenda's vagina) Philys, have you seen this forest?

Philys
Let me get my glasses on. Dilys, I've never seen anything like it. Not even Robin Hood could find his way through that forest.

Dilys

It must of took ages for her husband to find the right entrance.

Philys

I bet she has to hold that candle that burns at one end, so he could find his way up the dark passage.

Dilys

She would have to make sure the flame didn't get too close, or she would get singed.

Philys

With that amount of pubic hair, you would have to call the fire brigade before it burnt the house down.

Dilys

She definitely needs a Brazilian.

Philys

Let's face it Pele would have never found the back of the net with that forest in the way.

Dilys

Don't look at her toenails.

Philys

Dilys, if there is ever a woman that needs her nails painting, it's her.

Dilys

It would cover some of her fungal problems.

Philys

I dated a man once with terrible feet.

Dilys

Did you?

Philys

I did. His feet went a shade of green and his toes went black.

Dilys

That's not the best combination of colours. I had a one night stand once with a guy who had green and black wall paper.

Philys

How did that go?

Dilys

Not very well. It was like having sex in a field at night, with the snow falling down. The whole sexual experience left me very cold.

Philys

I bet it did.

Dilys

So what happened to his feet?

Philys

They had to get amputated. The shade of green was gangrene.

Dilys

What did you call him, stumpy?

Philys

He did has some prosthetic feet fitted, but because they were made of wood, I kept getting splinters. They kept snagging my tights.

Dilys

That's not good.

Philys

That's what I thought, so I dumped him. I moved out and the termites moved in.

Dilys

Mo, there is movement in the hedge row.

Mini Meg

Right Brenda, it is time to push.

Brenda

(Pushing and screaming) Mo!

Mo

Carol get hold of her other hand. Now push.

Five minutes later, Mini Meg delivers a baby girl, then a baby boy.

Brenda

Are they both alright?

Mini Meg

They are perfect. *(Mini Meg cleans the babies in the sink and passes them to Brenda)*

Brenda

(Crying) They are beautiful.

Mo

Like mother like children.

Philys

Meg love, I can see movement down below.

Mini Meg

(*Taking a look*) It's definitely round three.

Mo

Ladies take the babies. (*Phoebe takes the boy, Carol takes the girl*)

Carol

I might have known you would take the boy.

Mo

Not now Carol.

Mini Meg

Push Brenda push.

After another five minutes, another baby boy is born.

Brenda

Is the baby healthy?

Mo

This beautiful boy is healthy. (*Mo hands the baby to Brenda*)

Brenda

Mo, I've got triplets.

Mo

And everyone's healthy. You have been blessed this Christmas Brenda.

Brenda

(*Crying*) Happy Christmas Mo. What am I going to do with five children?

Mo

You are going to look after them and love them like any good mother would.

Brenda

How am I going to afford it?

Mo

With the help of friends and family of course. I'll pick up Tommy and Jenny from school. They can stop at mine tonight.

Brenda

Thank you.

Mo

That's what friends and family do.

Dick comes running into the hairdressers. Seeing Brenda holding three babies in her arms, he falls onto the floor.

Carol

Typical bloke. Always late coming and useless when he gets here.

As Brenda is lying there with her three babies, the choir comes up to the hairdressers window and start singing 'Away In A Manger'. The ambulances blue lights can be seen in the background.

Home for Christmas

Characters

Mo, Phoebe, Carol, Vera Virus, Janice, Mini Meg, Penny pick a nose, Pill Gill, Tina Tart, Duke and Duchess of Ruttingham, Lord Fircum, Pissed up Pete, Ron, Billy, Ben Hung, Harold, Mary, Gary, Dilys and Philys, The Fella Bella, Policeman Mickey, Sheila Ore, Dick, Tommy and Jenny, Angie, Michael, Dirty Kath and the night ladies, Stella, slaves, Bucket Bill and his wife, Bert and Tony.

Setting

The Manor House.

Home for Christmas

In the early evening, Mo comes out of her cottage and walks down the lane. She is wearing a long evening dress with an imitation fur coat covering it. She is also wearing a diamond tiara. As she gets to the gates of the Manor, she can see Phoebe and Janice waiting for her.

Mo
Good evening ladies.

They both curtsey.

Janice
You look beautiful Mo.

Mo
Thank you Janice.

Phoebe
That tiara looks as though it's worth a few quid. Where did you nick it from?

Mo
Phoebe Clarkson, you have got a corrupt mind.

Phoebe
It doesn't seem five minutes since I caught you nicking food. Now look at you.

Mo
You had a right go at me.

Phoebe
I'm not surprised. You were nicking the good stuff, that was

only out of date by a day.

Janice
Did life get that bad?

Mo
When you were sleeping on a park bench and didn't have a penny to your name, Phoebe's out of date food was like eating from Harrods Christmas hamper.

Phoebe
Now look at you, at the top of the social Christmas tree.

Janice
Would you do it all again?

Mo
Do you know Janice, I suffered so much anguish and pain in my life, but to see my son become a Duke, I would do it all again in a heart beat.

Phoebe
Who have we got first?

Mo
Miss Wonders and her slaves.

Pill Gill takes her slaves onto the grass with a megaphone in her hand she sings 'Thriller' with the slaves as her backing dancers.

Phoebe
Well, you don't see that everyday.

Janice
Those slaves have got next to nothing on, they must be freezing.

After the song, they all walk up to Mo, Pill Gill curtseys and the slaves bow.

Pill Gill

That song was dedicated to Your Ladyship, as it is a thrill to have you in all our lives.

Mo

Thank you Miss Wonders. Now off you all go and get warm.

Phoebe

Isn't the video about the dead rising from the grave?

Mo

Carry on and you will never rise again.

Phoebe

Talking about the living dead, here comes Lassie.

Dennis walks up to Mo and bows.

Dennis

You look amazing Your Ladyship.

Mo

Thank you Dennis. I've heard you have met someone and plan on getting married?

Dennis

I have Your Ladyship.

Mo

Congratulations. I hope you will be very happy together.

Dennis

Thank you Your Ladyship. *(He walks into the Manor)*

Phoebe

I heard they met on Dogging.com. I also heard her profile name was 'A bitch needs breeding.' Good luck with that bitch.

Janice

Is he still dogging?

Phoebe

He's like a dog with a bone, he just can't let it go. Someone was telling me the other week that he was walking around the woods frothing from the mouth. Apparently someone had phoned the police and told them to bring a gun as a dog was walking around the woods with rabies. When the police arrived they discovered he had been eating a 'lemon sherbet dip.' He has moved onto 'cough cough twists' now, because every time he coughs it sounds like a dog barking.

Mo

We will have to see if any puppies come from the marriage. *(They all laugh)*

Phoebe

Talking of dogs, here comes a couple of bitches.

Dog face Donna and Gemma Raud walk up to Mo. Donna bows and Gemma curtseys.

Dog face Donna

Hello Your Ladyship.

Mo

Good evening ladies. It's nice to see you both again. Is it a flying visit?

Gemma Raud

We are just here visiting my parents for Christmas. We don't like to leave the bar for too long.

Dog face Donna

We supply accommodation now as well. Bella emailed me to ask if she could book her wedding with us. Apparently there are some rare fruits on the island that Policeman Mickey hasn't tried before. You must all come out and join us for a couple of weeks.

Phoebe

That sounds wonderful Donna. Make sure you give me your email address later.

Dog face Donna

We will. *(They both walk into the Manor)*

Mo

How many faces have you brought with you this evening?

Phoebe

I don't know what you mean.

Janice

Where is their bar?

Mo

The Greek island of Lesves.

Phoebe

You should go Janice. Let's face it you don't have that much luck with men.

Janice

How rude.

Phoebe

Here comes your equals.

The Duke and Duchess of Ruttingham greet Mo.

The Duke
Your Ladyship.

Mo
Your Grace. *(Mo curtseys)*

The Duke
It's so nice to see you have reached the heights you deserve.
What a nice man your son is.

Mo
Thank you Your Grace.

The Duke
I know he will move the estate onto further greatness.

Mo
I'm sure he will Your Grace.

The Duke
Would you excuse me. *(He walks into the Manor)*

The Duchess
Mo, how are you?

Mo
I'm well Brenda. How's the garden coming along?

The Duchess
From strength to strength. The Duke has taken up gardening
himself. He has become an expert in pruning the bushes. But as
yet, he hasn't become an expert in restoration. So I have to bring
to the attention of the restoration staff what needs touching up.

Mo

Is the restoration work ongoing?

The Duchess

It never stops Mo. There is always something that needs attention. I'll see you later. *(She walks into the Manor)*

Lord Fircum

How wonderful to see you again.

Mo

It's always a pleasure Your Lordship.

Lord Fircum

Did you get my little present?

Mo

I did Your Lordship. Me and my husband have spent many hours of fun swinging up and down.

Lord Fircum

By the sounds of it, it was the right present to get you. Every time you ride it I hope it reminds you of the fun that is waiting for you at Fircum Hall.

Mo

I'm sure it won't be long before I'm swinging to your tune.

Lord Fircum

You will be like Lady Godiva riding a swing instead of a horse. Until we meet again. *(He kisses Mo's hand and walks into the Manor)*

Janice

What was that all about?

Mo

He brought me a swing, to remind me of his swinging parties at Fircum Hall. Ron grows his runner beans up it. *(They all laugh)*

Phoebe

With a plague of mosquitoes above her hand, it can only be one person.

Dirty Kath and the night ladies walk up to Mo and curtsey.

Mo

Good evening Kath.

Dirty Kath

Hello Your Ladyship.

Mo

I've heard you have invented a new pie?

Dirty Kath

Yes, it's called Blue Bottle Pie. It's made of natural ingredients. It is becoming very big in America.

Mo

Congratulations.

Dirty Kath

Thank you Your Ladyship. *(They all walk off into the Manor)*

Phoebe

Dirty bitch. The fly population has halved in her cafe since she started making those pies. The reason they are big in America is because the police and detectives threaten prisoners with Kath's pies when they are being interrogated. Not one of them have been able to hold out against the 'Blue Bottle Pie.' Even doctors are prescribing Kath's pie to their patients with obesity problems. The toilets are full so I've heard.

Mo

Thank you Phoebe love.

Janice

This is a first.

Zit faced Zita comes up the drive.

Mo

Good evening Zita.

Zit faced Zita

Good evening Your Ladyship. *(She curtseys)*

Mo

You are looking so well.

Zit faced Zita

Thank you Your Ladyship. I do feel first class.

Mo

I see you have lost your teenage spots.

Zit faced Zita

I tripped over a bottle of Clearsil when I was coming out of the Post Office one day. As you can see it's taken me from second to first class. *(She walks into the Manor)*

Phoebe

Stumbled. More like fell over the hundreds that had been thrown at her. What was that, 'I can see you have got rid of your teenage spots.' She is in her fifties.

Mo

Diplomacy Mrs Clarkson.

Phoebe

Taking the piss Mrs Johnson.

Mini Meg, Penny Pick a Nose and Stella walk up towards Mo.
They all curtsey.

Mo

Marvellous Meg, the giver of life.

Mini Meg

Thank you Your Ladyship. If it had been a gents hairdressers, she would of ended up delivering the babies herself.

Phoebe

Penny you look lovely. I can see you have put white tape on your fingers to match your outfit. You are becoming a fashion icon.

Penny Pick a Nose

Thank you Mrs Clarkson, Although I could never match your style.

Phoebe

How right you are.

Mo

We are looking forward to you joining us this Christmas.

Stella

Thank you Your Ladyship.

Mo

I have even heard you're four times more booked up for the next six months.

Stella

I can't imagine why.

Mo

I think it's due to the quality of your assets you are bringing with you.

Phoebe

More like the amount of porn men like looking at.

Mo

Get yourselves in and out of the cold. *(They walk into the Manor)*

Phoebe

Here comes Hinge and Bracket.

Mo

Ladies how nice to see you.

Dilys

Thank you Your Ladyship.

Philys

We took round some knitted baby things for those three beautiful babies earlier.

Mo

That was so kind of you both.

Dilys

We also took some waxing strips around as well. As Philys said, if Brenda is going to have that much activity going on around her front bottom, she will need to keep it neat and tidy at all times.

Mo

So thoughtful of you both.

Philys

That's what we thought. *(They both walk into the Manor)*

Phoebe

I've heard they have put a card in the post office window, letting themselves out as birthing partners.

Janice

I've heard everyone who reads the card says they can get knitted. *(They all laugh)* Now there's a man who I would knit underwear for.

The Mayor comes up the drive.

The Mayor

(Bowing) You look so regal Your Ladyship.

Mo

Thank you Your Worship. You know Mrs Clarkson, but I don't think you have met my dear friend Janice.

The Mayor

I don't think I have. *(He shakes her hand)*

Janice

It is a great honour to meet you Your Worship. *(She keeps shaking his hand)*

Mo

Are you alright Janice? There is steam coming out of your coat.

Janice

Would you excuse me please. *(She runs into the Manor)*

The Mayor

That reminds me. I must book my train ticket. *(He walks into the Manor)*

Phoebe

Well, I've heard people getting hot under the collar but never under the coat.

Bucket Bill and his wife greet Mo.

Mo

You made it Bill.

Bucket Bill

I didn't want to miss my last Christmas at the Manor. Look after him, Your Ladyship, and tell him I loved him very much.

Mo

I will Bill.

Bucket Bill

Although I have left my stall to my cousins, I'm sure he will let Billy work on it at weekends.

Mo

That is kind of you Bill, but it won't be the same without you being there.

Bucket Bill

What are your plans for Billy?

Mo

With my son now a Duke, his estate will need someone to take care of the gardens.

Bucket Bill

So he will go from selling fruit and veg, to growing it.

Mo

Something like that.

Bucket Bill

He will do an excellent job. Goodbye Your Ladyship.

Mo

Goodbye Bill.

Bucket Bill and his wife go into the Manor.

Phoebe

Very sad.

Mo

That's one thing I won't enjoy next year.

Phoebe

What's that?

Mo

Taking Billy to his Dad's funeral.

Phoebe

Here comes the Ore's.

The Fella Bella, Policeman Mickey and Sheila Ore walk up to Mo and curtsey, with Policeman Mickey bowing.

Mo

Hello everyone.

Sheila Ore

You won't believe it.

Mo

What?

Sheila Ore

They have barred me from the pub.

Mo

No.

Sheila Ore

They have. All I did was make the customers feel welcome.

Mo

You were always hands on Sheila.

Sheila Ore

I was. It was me who gave the men my time and patience in fixing their brewers droops. It was because of me their wives found their husband's manhoods in full working order.

Mo

It's their loss.

Sheila Ore

You are so right.

Mo

I've heard it's Greece for the wedding.

The Fella Bella

Finally, we have both found a place we both like. You are coming out to be with us on our big day.

Mo
Of course. I wouldn't miss it for the world.

The Fella Bella
We will see you later. *(They all walk into the Manor)*

Phoebe
It serves her right, the dirty old tart, and as for you sticking up for her, what face have you brought with you tonight?

Mo
How rude.

Phoebe
If you think you are going to the Greek Islands without me, think again.

Janice walks back from the Manor.

Mo
Feeling better love?

Janice
I just got a bit steamed up.

Phoebe
I bet you won't be taking your coat off tonight.

Mo
Here comes the father of five.

Tommy and Jenny come running up to Mo, with Dick walking behind.

Tommy/Jenny
Aunty Mo. *(They all hug)*

Mo

Hello you two. Hello Dick (he bows) have you left her?

Dick

It was her idea. With the babies sleeping she wanted some time with her waxing strips. Everyone has been so generous.

Mo

That's what families do.

Dick

I'm sorry we didn't get you presents this Christmas. With three extra, we couldn't afford it.

Mo

Dick, you have already given us our presents. You brought three new lives into our family. The Duke got another tip off, about a horse that was running in the two o'clock at Sanddown. So me, Ron and the Duke put a bet on for you. It came in as fifty to one. *(She passes him an envelope)* Put the thousand pounds somewhere safe.

Dick

Thank you so much. *(Tears start to fall down his cheeks)*

Mo

Also, that job you hate so much, you need to hand in your notice. The Duke wants to see you after New Year's so he can talk to you about working on the estate. Merry Christmas Dick.

Dick

Merry Christmas Your Ladyship.

Mo

Now off you go and get your two a drink.

He walks into the Manor with Tommy and Jenny.

Janice

This village needs to erect a statue of you.

Phoebe

It will give the pigeons something to work on.

Mo

You are a bitter bitch.

Phoebe

You're right. It's bitter cold out here. They say snow is on its way. Now there's a woman I've not seen in a while.

Tina Tart and her friend Angie come up to Mo. They both curtsey.

Tina

Hello Your Ladyship.

Mo

Hello Tina. Have you been keeping well?

Tina Tart

Very well thank you. This is my close friend Angie.

Mo

How nice to meet you.

Tina Tart

It has taken me all these years, but I've finally become a vegetarian.

Mo

Meat can give you jaw ache with all that chewing.

Tina Tart

Now I've moved on from jaw ache to tongue ache.

Both Tina and Angie walk into the Manor.

Phoebe

You don't see that everyday.

Harold and Mary come up the driveway. Harold bows and greets everyone with a kiss. Mary curtseys.

Mo

Hello you gorgeous girl.

Mary

Hello Aunty Mo.

Mo

Everything alright?

Mary

Everything is great Aunty Mo.

Mo

(To Harold) Just the two of you then?

Harold

Simon is arriving tomorrow.

Mo

I'll expect you all for Christmas dinner.

Phoebe

It looks like you are going to have your mouth full of meat this Christmas.

Harold

It's a good job I've not gone vegetarian. *(They all laugh)*

Harold and Mary walk into the Manor.

Janice

It wouldn't be Christmas If Carol and Tony weren't arguing.

Carol

I'm not bothered how good your veg is this year. *(Carol curtseys and gives Mo a kiss)*

Tony

(Bowing) Don't you think the Duke might want my veg for Christmas dinner Your Ladyship?

Carol

No he wouldn't.

Tony

But my carrots are outstanding this year, they look just like your legs.

Phoebe

Are you sure they are that outstanding?

Carol

Bitch. *(To Phoebe)* Carry on and you will find my legs around your throat.

Mo

I'll tell you what, I'll have a word with the cook. I'll tell you what he says.

Carol

Thank you Mo.

Phoebe

How did you get on with the bank manager?

Carol

He's a dirty old man. I sat down and his eyes were all over me like a rash. I dropped my purse as you said, but when I went to pick it up one of my boobs fell out.

Phoebe

Just one?

Carol

One's enough, believe me. Anyway, the next minute he was giving me so many financial benefits I couldn't believe my ears.

Vera Virus and Bert walk over.

Vera Virus

(She curtseys and Burt bows) What's going on here then?

Phoebe

We are talking about Carols trip to see the bank manager.

Vera Virus

The dirty old man. I sat down and dropped my pen and as I went to pick it up both my boobs fell out. He gave me half the financial benefits that she got.

Phoebe

Yes but your two don't match up to her one. In fact, it's a good job you never went in for breast feeding.

Vera Virus

Cheeky cow.

Phoebe

You need to get your Bert to put his hands on them more.

Bert

You see our Vera, every time you say no, it's costing us money.

Vera Virus

My tits are as good as anybody else's. You don't complain when you have ran out of milk for your cornflakes in a morning.

Carol

They look fine to me.

Vera Virus

Thank you Carol. *(They both walk into the Manor with their husbands walking behind them)*

Pissed up Pete can be seen walking sideways at the bottom of the lawn.

Janice

Is that Pissed up Pete who likes it neat?

Mo

It looks like it, he's down. *(Pete falls over)*

Phoebe

He's up.

Janice

No he's down. Where's Her Grace?

Mo

She is already in the Manor. She is playing the hostess with the mostess. She was telling me earlier that because the Manor is so big, she has lost her way around several times and ended up in the butler's cupboard.

Phoebe
It's better than the closet.

Mo
Well I think it's time we went in.

Phoebe
Where's your Ron?

Mo
He's babysitting Billy. Where's your Ben?

Phoebe
He is doing the same thing with Gary.

Janice
Are they really? Who are these people coming up the drive?

They both turn around.

Mo
Wait till I get my hands on him.

Billy
Aunty Mo.

Gary
Aunty Phoebe.

They both run up and hug each of their parents.

Mo
(To Ron) What's your excuse?

Ron

Billy made me come.

Mo

So what did a ten year old boy do, threaten to beat you up?

Ron

Well I told you not to let him watch WWE wrestling. So it's your fault.

Mo

It would be me wouldn't it. I just hope you can wrestle with being in the spare room tonight.

Ron

(Kissing Mo on the cheek) Happy Christmas beautiful.

Mo

(Trying not to smile) Can you escort Janice into the Manor?

Ron

Nothing would give me greater pleasure. *(They walk into the Manor arm in arm)*

Phoebe

I hope your jobs are all done?

Ben Hung

Me and Gary did them together. Although there is one job left that I need to do.

Phoebe

Is there?

Ben Hung

I've missed something in the bedroom.

Phoebe

I think we need to talk about this some more. *(All three of them walk into the Manor)*

Mo is left standing on her own. After watching Pissed up Pete falling over several times, she spots Michael walking through the gates. He waves as he walks up to her.

Mo

Hello Your Grace.

Michael

Good evening my beautiful Mother.

Mo

You're home at last.

Peterson comes out of the Manor with two glasses of Champagne that are carried on a silver tray. As they toast each other, all the guests assemble at the front of the Manor and raise their glasses. The fireworks light up the sky.

Self Reflection